THE GUNSMITH

437

The Reluctant Executioner

Books by J.R. Roberts
(Robert J. Randisi)

The Gunsmith series
Books 1 - 220

The Lady Gunsmith series
Books 1 - 5

Angel Eyes series
Books 1 - 4

Tracker series
Books 1 - 4

Mountain Jack Pike series
Books 1 - 4

COMING SOON!

The Gunsmith
438 – The Treasure of Little Bighorn

For more information visit:
www.speakingvolumes.us

THE GUNSMITH

437

The Reluctant Executioner

J.R. Roberts

SPEAKING VOLUMES, LLC
NAPLES, FLORIDA
2018

The Reluctant Executioner

ISBN 978-1-62815-861-8

Chapter One

Shots in the Nebraska distance attracted the attention of Clint Adams, the Gunsmith. In the past, not minding his own business had caused Clint much grief, but also a little satisfaction. He found, picking back through his memories, the gratification usually outweighed the grief.

So he had no choice but to ride toward the sound to see what was going on.

There was no problem finding where the shots were coming from, because they continued as he approached. To his trained ear it sounded like more than a few guns being fired— possibly as many as half a dozen.

As he rode to the top of a hill he saw the tableau spread out below him. One man was crouched down behind an overturned wagon. He was returning fire as 4 or 5 men—he couldn't see quite clearly from his vantage point—were firing at him. All the shooting was being done with rifles.

Clint didn't know the circumstances of the firefight. The one man could have been a criminal surrounded by a posse. Or, he was an innocent being attacked by would be bandits. The only thing Clint knew was that one man was being fired on by many, and that didn't sit well with him.

But before he took a hand he needed a better look. If the group was a posse, there'd be a man with a badge among them. He decided to try to get a better look at the men, perhaps good enough to enable him to spot a badge.

He changed position, so that instead of eyeing the activity from behind the lone man, he was to the side, where he could see that man as well as the others a little more clearly. There were 5 of them, having taken cover behind some rocks. Clint had a folding spyglass in his saddlebag, which he took out and used to get a better look. As he watched the 5 men stood, fired, and then ducked behind their cover, again. He saw them fairly clearly, but was not able to see a badge. Of course, that didn't mean they weren't a posse, but he felt that a posse would be doing more than simply firing, they'd be trying to get the man to surrender so they could bring him in. Of course, that was assuming it wasn't a lynch mob.

He turned his spyglass to the single man crouching behind his overturned wagon. A robber would not be fleeing from a posse in what looked like a drummer's wagon. But he had obviously been on the run, because Clint could see deep ruts made by the wheels just before the wagon had flipped. The man was hatless, didn't look to be wearing a holster, and didn't seem too seriously injured by the fall. And, even from this distance, Clint could tell that the man was not at all familiar with firing his rifle.

He decided the man needed help.

From the way things were going, the firefight could have gone on all day, depending on how many bullets they all had. It was more likely that the man behind the wagon would run out of ammo first, which might have been what the 5 were depending on.

Clint could have ridden up behind the fallen wagon, dismounted and taken up position alongside the man, to try to fight the 5 off, but he decided to take a more direct action.

He mounted Eclipse, stowed the spyglass away, took out his rifle, and started riding straight at the 5 men, from the side.

He started to fire, but was careful not to hit anyone, since he still didn't know who the men were. His lead struck the rocks, sending sparks and slivers of stone flying, surprising the men. They turned, saw him coming, and had to shift position to take cover behind the rocks. However, this made them vulnerable to the shots being fired by the man they were attacking. In effect, they were in a crossfire, and could not take cover against both.

Their horses were behind them, tied so they wouldn't bolt. 2 men gave it up instantly, sprinted for their horses and fled. The other 3 made a show of exhibiting some courage, but as Clint came closer, as did his shots, they followed the lead of their colleagues, ran for their horses and rode off.

Clint stopped firing and rode toward the man and the fallen wagon. Warily, the man stood and waited.

"Are you okay?" Clint asked.

"I think so," the man said. "I'll be some sore, I guess, but I'll live."

"Why don't we get this wagon up so you can assess the damage."

"I appreciate the help," the man said. "My name's Carlton Wainwright."

"Clint Adams," Clint said, dismounting.

In the end Clint had to hunt down the man's horse, which hadn't run off too far. They then used it and Eclipse to get the wagon up on its wheels, which didn't seem to be broken.

"Looks to be in good shape," Clint commented.

"It's well-built," Wainwright said. "Should be okay."

He and Clint examined his horse, next.

"He seems all right," Clint said. "I can't see any injuries." He looked at Wainwright, a tall, rangy man in his 40s.

"It's gettin' dark," the man said. "Will you camp with me?"

"I guess that depends."

"On what?"

"On what you did to make those men want to kill you," Clint explained.

"Oh," Wainwright said, "well, it's not so much what I did. As what I'm gonna do, I guess."

"What do you mean?"

Wainwright walked to the back of his wagon and reached inside.

"Everythin' got tossed around back here—ah, here it is," he said.

As he withdrew his hands Clint saw what he was holding. It was a rope, tied into a hangman's noose.

"I can only suppose it has somethin' to do with this," Wainwright said. "You see, I'm a hangman-an executioner. I'm on my way to a town called Fate, Nebraska to hang a man."

"And you figure they were trying to stop you?"

"That's all I can figure," Wainwright said. "I ain't done anythin' else to make anybody that mad."

"Well," Clint said, "let's make camp and maybe we can figure it out over coffee and beans."

Chapter Two

By the time they picketed the horses, built a fire and got the coffee and food going, it was dark. They sat near the fire, with Wainwright looking round then, nervously.

"Do you suppose they'd try to come back after dark?" he asked.

"I doubt it," Clint said. "Maybe if they were a posse."

"Not a posse," Wainwright said. "Omigod, you think maybe they were lawmen?"

"I doubt that," Clint said. "They could've been trying to rob you."

"Maybe, but they started yellin' at me when they rode up," Wainwright said.

"What were they saying?"

"I'm not sure."

"Has this ever happened to you before?" Clint asked. "People from town trying to run you off?"

"No," Wainwright said, "but—you're the Gunsmith, right?"

"That's right."

"I thought so," the hangman said. "When you introduced yourself, I thought—maybe you can help me."

"Do you want me to ride into Fate with you?"

"Actually," Wainwright said, "I was hopin' maybe you'd ride into Fate *for* me."

"What?"

"I mean," the man said, "you've killed before, you been to hangings, right? You know how it's done."

"You want me to take your place?" Clint asked.

"Well," Wainwright said, "it's just somethin' that occurred to me—"

"When?"

"Just now," the man said, "but . . ."

"Is this because they were shooting at you?" Clint asked. "I can ride in with you, make sure you don't get shot at, again. When we get to town we can talk to the sheriff—"

Clint stopped because he thought the hangman wasn't listening to him.

"Carlton!"

The man shook his head as if coming out of a dream and looked at him.

"Just call me Carl."

"Carl, what's wrong?"

"I've been doin' this for a long time," he explained. "All of a sudden . . . it bothers me."

"Why did you start?" Clint asked. "How long ago?"

Wainwright hesitated a moment.

"I have a bottle of whiskey in my wagon—if it didn't get broken. Will you have a drink with me?"

"Sure," Clint said, "although I'd just as soon put it in my coffee."

"I'll get it."

Wainwright got up, went to his wagon and came back with half a bottle of whiskey. He poured some into Clint's cup, and then did the same for himself. He put the bottle aside and sat across the fire from Clint, again.

"This is somethin' I've been strugglin' with only recently," he said, finally. "Those men attackin' me, shoutin'. . ." He trailed off.

"What is it?"

"It just came to me what they were shoutin' at me when they rode up."

"What was it?"

"'Hangman, go home,'" Wainwright said.

"Well then," Clint said, "I guess there's no doubt why they were attacking you. But were they out to scare you away, or actually kill you?"

"Once my wagon turned over I believe they were tryin' to kill me," Wainwright said.

"Then don't go to Fate," Clint said. "Go somewhere else and send a telegram explaining."

"I can't do that," Wainwright said. "I've never shirked my responsibilities."

"This is different," Clint said. "Somebody tried to kill you."

"I can't just run," he said. "I mean . . . I was running when the wagon turned over. But that's not the kind of runnin' I mean."

"I understand that," Clint said. "But . . . this has been such a part of your life for so long, now. Why would it start to bother you?"

"I have no idea," Wainwright said. "I've just started having . . . dreams."

"About . . . the people you've hanged?"

"No faces," Wainwright said. "I don't remember no faces. They come to me . . . hooded."

"And what do they say?"

"Nothin'," the hangman said. "They just . . . stare."

"After all this time?"

Wainwright shrugged, poured some more whiskey into his now empty cup.

"You never answered me," Clint said. "How long's it been?"

"Thirty years," Wainwright said, "I've been an executioner for thirty years."

Chapter Three

"I needed somethin'," Wainwright said. "When I was younger, springin' a trap door under a hooded figure seemed a pretty easy way to make a livin'."

"Doesn't sound easy," Clint said.

"If you don't look at them as people," Wainwright said, "then it's not a problem. But . . . lately I've started to look at them. That's where my trouble started."

"So make this your last one," Clint suggested.

"And then what do I do?" Wainwright asked. "It's a little late in life to look for a new profession, don't you think?"

"Don't hangmen ever retire?" Clint asked.

"Do gunfighters ever retire?" Wainwright asked.

"They try."

"And men still come after them—you, right?"

"It's been known to happen."

"People don't like executioners," Wainwright said. "They sure as hell don't want one livin' in their town."

"So what do you want to do?" Clint asked.

"Well," Wainwright said, "first I have to get this next job done."

"Without getting yourself killed, right?"

"Exactly."

"Who are you hanging?" Clint asked.

"A man named Dave Miklin."

"Do you know anything about him?"

"Just his name."

"So you don't know why a town would have five men who'd rather kill you than have him hanged?"

"Not a clue."

"You never get a man's history before you hang him?"

"I don't want to know him that well," the hangman said. I only want his name, the name of the town, and when he's to be executed."

"When is this one supposed to swing?"

"Two days," Wainwright said. "I always get to town early enough to check the facilities—the gallows."

"Or the tree they want you to use."

"In the old days, yes," Wainwright agreed. "These days I pretty much work with gallows."

"If the town bothers to build a gallows, why would they try to stop you?"

"Could just be friends of the prisoner," Wainwright said. "Though, if that was true, I'd rather they try to break him out than kill me. I mean, another execution date will simply be assigned."

"Maybe killing you would give them the time they need to break him out," Clint offered.

"Well," the hangman said, "I have two things to do in the next few days."

"And they are?"

"Complete this assignment," Wainwright said, "and then reevaluate my position. How can I continue this way if those prisoners keep coming in my dreams? And I'd like to stay alive long enough to get both of those things done."

"That doesn't seem to be too much to ask for," Clint commented.

"So, will you come with me?" Wainwright asked. "Keep me alive? I'll pay you. I can't pay much, but I'll give you what they're payin' me."

"No need," Clint said. "I don't like ambushers. I'll ride in with you and we'll talk to the law. I think I might be able to recognize one or two of the shooters."

"I will, too," Wainwright said. "They got pretty close to me before they started yellin' and shootin'."

"Let's get some rest, then," Clint said, "and get an early start. I'll stand watch."

Chapter Four

Wainwright insisted on also standing watch, so Clint took the first, and Wainwright the second.

In the morning they made do with coffee and beef jerky for breakfast, then got Eclipse saddled, the wagon hitched and got going.

Clint kept a wary eye out for another ambush. It was possible the 5 men went back to Fate, and decided to come out today with 10. He had the hangman keep his rifle across his thighs while he drove his rig.

"If it happens," he told him, "we don't want them getting too close."

"I understand."

"And don't shoot unless I say so," Clint added. "Just in case the town sends a welcoming committee."

But during the more than 10 miles ride to town they didn't run into anyone, shooting at them or welcoming them.

"Why are you doin' this?" Wainwright asked as they approached town.

"Doing what?"

"Helpin' me," the hangman said. "You don't even know me."

"I know I didn't like what was happening to you yesterday," Clint responded. "I just want to make sure it doesn't happen again."

"Were you headed for Fate, anyway?" Wainwright asked.

"Fate?" Clint replied, keeping his head turned. "I never heard of it until yesterday, when you mentioned it."

***

Fate was a small town, obviously with growing pains. Even as they approached Clint could smell newly cut wood, and see the partially erected structures of new buildings. Closer till and they could hear hammering and sawing of wood.

As they rode down the main street they attracted attention, but for once Clint didn't think it was him. It was the man driving the wagon next to him, as the town was expecting the arrival of an executioner. The wooden sides of Wainwright's wagon were blank, but that didn't stop people from staring. Word must have gotten back to town about the failed ambush attempt of the day before.

Halfway through town they came to a square, with buildings on four sides, and one street going left and one to the right, forming a Y. In the center was a newly erected gallows. Clint had no doubt that the fresh wood it had been constructed from would be refurbished afterward, and incorporated into a new building.

Wainwright reined his horse in. Clint stopped Eclipse next to him. They stared at the gallows while citizens walked by and stared at them.

"You want to get settled?" Clint asked. "Horse and wagon at the livery, get a hotel room?"

"I think I better check in with the sheriff. Why don't you get yourself a room?"

"I'll go along with you," Clint said. "Just to make sure you make it."

"Thanks."

"I think I see his office up that street," Clint said.

"I see it," Wainwright said. "There's a hanging shingle with a badge on it. Guess he really wants people to know where he is."

They took the street to the left and came to a stop in front of the sheriff's shingle. Somebody had done a nice job painting the badge on it.

Wainwright climbed down, Clint dismounted, and then stepped up to the office door.

"You gonna knock?" the hangman asked.

"Why?" Clint asked. "It's a public office."

"I don't know," Wainwright said with a shrug. "I always knock on a closed door."

"Well, we're here for you," Clint said. "Go ahead and knock."

Wainwright knocked, and then opened the door.

A man with a badge was coming around from behind the desk, probably to see who was knocking on his door. He stopped short as Wainwright and Clint walked in.

He was tall, in his 30s, well dressed, with a brown jacket, his badge pinned to a vest. In fact, he might have been the most well-dressed lawman Clint had ever seen—except for the Earps.

"Help you gents?"

"I'm Wainwright," the executioner said. "The hangman."

"Oh! That's good." He stuck his hand out. "Sheriff Hastings."

"Sheriff." They shook hands.

"And you?" the sheriff asked, looking at Clint. "Do, uh, hangmen have assistants?"

"This one does," Clint said. "I'm Clint Adams."

"Clint . . . Adams?"

"That's right."

"The Gunsmith."

"Right again."

"Jesus," the lawman said, surprised. "What's the Gunsmith doin' with a hangman?"

"Keeping him alive long enough for him to do his job."

"Whataya mean?"

"Five men ambushed him, tried to kill him. Probably from this town."

"Wait, what makes you think they'd be from this town?"

"Where else would they come from?" Clint asked. "What other reason would 5 men bushwhack him?"

"To rob him, maybe?"

"They yelled 'hangman, go home,'" Clint said. "What do you think that means?"

"I don't know what to say," the sheriff replied. "I know the decision to hang Dave Miklin wasn't a popular one here, but that was the judge's ruling. I have to abide by it."

"What about the rest of the town?" Wainwright asked.

"I can't speak for everyone else," Hastings said. "I just have to uphold the law in Fate."

"And the judge?" Wainwright asked. "Is he still here?"

"We're too small to have a judge here permanently," Hastings said. "He was a circuit judge. He heard the case, passed judgment, and left town."

"Very convenient," Clint said.

"Look," Hastings said, "nobody's come to me with any kind of threats to stop the hanging."

"There's been no talk in town of breaking him out?" Clint asked.

"Not that I've heard," Hastings said. "And if anyone tries, I'll stop 'em."

"Now do you feel about this hangin', Sheriff?" Wainwright asked.

"It don't matter how I feel," the man said.

"I'd like to know why this fellow is being hanged," Clint said. "What he did, and why the town is so up in arms about it?"

"I actually don't want to hear any of that," Wainwright said. "I try not to get to know the men I hang—beyond measuring and weighing them, that is."

"Why don't I see you to your hotel," Clint said, "and then I can come back and talk more with the sheriff."

"I have my rounds to do," Sheriff Hastings said, "but we can talk afterward."

"That's fine," Clint said.

"And I'll come by tomorrow for the prisoner's measurements," Wainwright said.

"I'll see what I can find out about the men who ambushed you," Hastings said. "I don't like bushwhackers."

"At least," Clint said, "we have that in common."

17

Chapter Five

Clint and Wainwright followed Sheriff Hastings' directions to a livery stable, where they left their horses and the hangman's wagon in the care of an elderly hostler, who had opinions about the hanging.

"Can't happen soon enough to suit me," he said, sourly.

"Is that the way most people feel about it?" Clint asked.

"Hell, no!" the man snapped. "That youngster Miklin is well liked hereabouts."

"So he's a nice fella?" Clint asked.

"He's arrogant, rude and conceited," the hostler said.

"Then why is he so well-liked?" Clint asked.

"His daddy's the biggest rancher in this area," the old man said. "That's why Miklin thought he could get away with murder."

"Is his father the type of man who would try to stop the hanging?" Clint asked.

"You bet he is," the hostler said. He looked at Wainwright. "You better watch out for him."

"I will," the hangman said.

"What's his name?" Clint asked.

"Henry Miklin."

"Thanks for the information," Clint said. "Why do you have such a dislike for them?"

"His old man is tryin' to buy me out, and I won't sell," the man said. "He can buy the whole town, but not my business."

Clint looked around. The stable was large, in the need of some repairs.

"Looks like it could do with a little work," Clint said.

"Can't we all," the man said, "but I can't afford it. Carpenters around here mostly work for Miklin, and their prices are high." He shrugged. "Just part of him tryin' to force me out."

"What's your name, sir?" Clint asked.

"Sam Holcroft."

"Well, Sam," Clint said, "maybe we can talk about getting this work done. I hate big ranchers who try to flex their muscle with their money."

"And their kids!" Holcroft said.

"Seems to me you might need a loan," Clint said, "or an investor."

"Mister, you come right on back and we'll talk over a drink," Holcroft said, happily.

"Deal," Clint said.

"What'd you say your name was?" Holcroft asked.

"Clint Adams."

As he and Wainwright walked out, carrying their gear, Clint heard Holcroft said, "Well, Jesus Christ!"

Chapter Six

Clint and Wainwright both registered at the Fate Inn. The hangman's room would be paid for by the town.

"Get some rest," Clint said. "Stay off the street, and watch who you open your door to."

"What are you gonna do?" Wainwright asked.

"Talk to the sheriff again," Clint said. "See if he found out anything about the ambush."

"And then?"

"I'll come back here for you and we'll get something to eat."

"That sounds great," Wainwright said, "but are you gonna go everywhere with me?"

"Right up until you hang Dave Miklin," Clint said. "You got a problem with that?"

"Not even a little one."

"Just make sure you keep your door locked," Clint cautioned. "And stay away from the window. Understand?"

"Got it," Wainwright said.

"I'll see you later."

***

Even though the sheriff said he had to make his rounds, Clint checked the office first. The door was unlocked, but the lawman was not inside. Instead of waiting there for him, he decided to walk around town to see if he ran into him. He also figured to keep his eyes and ears open for anything about the hanging.

When he walked for an hour without encountering the lawman—and virtually seeing the entire town—he retraced his steps and stopped in the Oak Lodge Saloon, across the street from the sheriff's office.

The place was mid-sized, fairly busy but not bustling. Men were seated with their whiskey or beer, and a few were standing at the bar. There were two saloon girls in the place, standing off to one side, having a conversation and looking bored. When Clint walked in they perked up, probably thinking of him as fresh meat.

As he approached the bar the two girls—a blonde and a brunette—exchanged some quick words, and then the brunette came over to him while the blonde looked unhappy.

"What'll ya have?" the bartender asked.

"Beer."

"Right."

As the girl reached him, the bartender set the beer in front of Clint.

"What about me?" she asked him, smiling.

"What about you?"

"Buy me a drink?"

"As long as it's not champagne," he said.

She laughed.

"We don't have any champagne here," she said. "Walt, I'll have a whiskey."

"Comin' up, Gina."

"You just get to town?" she asked Clint.

"A little while ago," he said.

"Do you know anybody?"

"I've only met the sheriff," he said. "Does he come in here a lot?"

"Oh, he's in and out all day," she said, taking her whiskey from the bartender. "Maybe you'd like to get to know more people?" she asked.

"Do you have anyone in mind?" he asked.

"Sure I do," she said. "Me." She put her hand out for him to shake "I'm Gina."

"I'm Clint," he said, shaking it.

"That's Rusty, over there," Gina said, indicating the blonde. "She's upset."

"Is she? About what?"

"When you came in I had to remind her it was my turn."

"Your turn for what?"

"To meet the new man in town," she said. "I'm the welcoming committee."

"Well, I couldn't ask for a nicer one," Clint said, and they drank to that. "Another drink?"

"Sure," she said. "One more. Walt?"

"Comin' up," Walt said.

He set them both up again.

"So," Clint said, to Gina, "tell me something about this town."

"What do you want to know?"

"Just conversation," Clint said. "What's been going on?"

"Well, lately," she said, "all anyone can talk about is the upcoming hanging,"

"Hanging?" Clint Said. He took a drink so he wouldn't look overly interested in the subject. "Who's being hanged?"

"A local boy named Dave Miklin," she said. "His father's a big rancher round here."

"What did he do?"

"Shot and killed somebody," she said. "Actually, a friend of his. Supposedly, they were fighting over a girl."

"You?"

"Me? Oh, no," she said, "and not Rusty, either. This was a nice girl."

"Oh?"

"Oh yeah," she said. "Nobody fights over saloon girls. They fight over somebody they can't have."

"And who was that?"

"Her name's Evelyn Hargrove," Gina said.

"What does she do?"

"She's a pretty little kid, sixteen," Gina said, "lives with her father. She's sweet. We're kind of friends, even though I'm . . . a little older."

"So how does the town feel about this hanging? Are they looking forward to it, like most towns do?" he asked.

"Do they?"

"Well, as a spectacle," he said. "Some towns view it as a reason to party."

"Around here they're kind of mixed," she said. "Some in favor, some against."

"Who's in favor?" he asked.

"Most of the people in here," she said. "And the nice, decent people are against it."

Clint wondered if "nice, decent people" would go out to ambush the hangman?

"So?" she asked.

"So what?"

"You want to come upstairs?" she invited. "To my room, for a poke?"

"How much?" he asked.

"For you? Two dollars."

"I don't think so."

"A dollar?"

"I don't usually pay for sex, Gina," he said. "I'm really sorry."

"You don't?" she asked. "Or you don't have to? No, don't tell me. Maybe I'll find out for myself."

As she started away he asked, "So, is Rusty going to come over and try, now?"

"Do you want her to?" she asked. "Maybe you prefer blondes?"

"No, that's not it," he said.

"Okay, then," she said. "I'll tell her you're not interested. But that doesn't mean she won't try."

As Gina walked back over to Rusty and spoke to her, Clint turned and saw Sheriff Hastings come in through the bat wing doors. When the lawman spotted him at the bar he walked over to him.

Chapter Seven

"Beer?" Clint asked.

"Thanks," Hastings said, waving to the bartender.

"I've been hearing that the townspeople are pretty mixed about this hanging."

Accepting the beer from the bartender, the lawman said, "If you're listening to people in here, you'd think they were in favor of it."

"But the nice people in town?"

"The decent people are against it," he said. "They're the people who feel that Old Man Miklin might pull his businesses out of town if we hang his son."

"Ah," Clint said, "I get it. Did you hear anything about the ambush?"

"No, nothin'," Hastings said. "But I'm not done lookin' into it."

"Neither am I," Clint said.

"It's my job," the lawman said. "Why are you involved? Are you friends with Mr. Wainwright?"

"Just met him today," Clint said.

"Then why are you so determined to keep him alive?" Hastings asked.

"I don't like bushwhackers," Clint said. "It's been tried on me many times and I don't usually let people get away with it."

"So you kill them."

"Well, I make sure they pay," Clint said, "one way or another."

"And that's what you wanna do now?"

"Yes."

"So I suppose you think I should deputize you?"

"Oh, God, no," Clint said. "I wore a badge years ago. I don't need one."

"I can't have you runnin' around here dispensing your own brand of justice," the lawman said.

"I just intend to keep Wainwright alive so he can do his job," Clint said. "And if somebody tries to kill him, I'm going to stop them."

"So if you find out who it was," Hastings said, "you'll come to me, right?"

"That's right."

"Good."

"Unless I find them in the act."

"Well," Hastings said, "you've two days to keep him alive. That means you'll have to stick to him the whole time."

"I can do that," Clint said.

"He's alone now, though," Hastings pointed out.

"Locked in his hotel room," Clint said. "And I'm going over there right now. We're going to have supper. Any suggestions?"

Chapter Eight

Clint knocked on the door of Carlton Wainwright's room. When the man answered he looked nervous.

"Jesus," he said, "I've been jumping at every noise in the hall."

"You don't have to jump anymore," Clint said. "Come on, let's get something to eat."

"Good, I'm starving."

They went down through the lobby and out onto the street.

"Where can we eat?" Wainwright asked.

"The sheriff recommended a place to me," Clint said. "It's right down the street."

By the time they got there it was starting to get dark out. The inside was well lit, and they could hear the sound of silverware against plates.

On the window it said STEAKHOUSE. Nothing else. Inside was surprisingly large for a town so small, many tables, most of which were taken at that time. But there were some empties, mostly in the rear, which suited Clint.

A waiter showed them to one and took their orders for steak dinners.

A look around the room told them that many of the diners knew who one or both of them were.

"What have you found out, so far?" Wainwright asked.

Clint explained that the town was split, but that it was likely the people in that restaurant were among those who were
against the hanging.

"They're afraid that the rancher, Miklin, will pull out,"
Clint said. "That would cripple the town's growth."

"I can't be faulted for that," Wainwright said. "I can't even
be concerned with it. I just have to do my job."

"That's right."

"If I can."

"Now, Mr. Wainwright—"

"You can call me Carlton," he said, "or Carl."

"All right," Clint said, "and I'm Clint. Are you saying you
might not be able to hang this man?"

"I—I don't know," Wainwright said. "I guess that will de-
pend on what happens the next two nights."

"Meaning dreams?"

Wainwright nodded.

"Tomorrow I'll take his statistics, and inspect the gallows."

"But it's what comes next you might have trouble with,"
Clint observed.

"Yes."

"Well," Clint said, "you have two days to figure it out."

When their dinners came Clint noticed that the dreams and
doubts the hangman was having apparently did not affect his
appetite.

Over desert of coffee and pie Wainwright said, "Usually
when I come to a town I stop in the saloon on the first night
and have a drink."

"Why is that?"

"I try to show the people I'm human, and not some kind of ghoul."

"Okay," Clint said, "when we finish here we'll go and have a drink."

"Yes, but what if the bushwhackers are in the saloon?"

"If they are," Clint said, "we'll deal with them."

***

Clint and Wainwright walked to the Oak Lodge Saloon, which was much busier than it had been when Clint was last there. The saloon girls, Gina and Rusty, were moving about the floor, delivering drinks and dodging the groping hands of customers.

There was just enough room at the bar for Clint and the hangman to grab a space.

"Two beers," Clint told the bartender.

"Right."

He set two ice cold mugs in front of them. Clint picked his up and looked around, while Wainwright lifted his, staring ahead into the mirror.

"If you don't turn around they can't see your face," Clint commented.

"I know," Wainwright said. "I'm workin' up to it. I'm just afraid someone will open fire."

"Well, if that happens we'll get this out in the open," Clint said, "find out who the ambushers were."

"I'd like to do that without gettin' killed," the hangman sad.

"Finish your beer, and then we'll head on back to the hotel. Maybe we'll be able to find something out tomorrow without any shots being fired."

Wainwright turned his head and looked at Clint.

"With your reputation how can you come into a place like this, with so many guns, and be calm?"

"My reputation convinces more people to give me a wide berth than it does to step up and try me," Clint said.

"What about ambushers?"

"I've had my fair share, but that mostly happens outside, not inside."

Chapter Nine

Clint walked Wainwright back to the hotel and to his door.

"What are you gonna do?" the hangman asked.

"I'm going to my room, too. Right down the hall. Number seven. If you need anything just knock on my door."

"I probably won't," Wainwright said. "I'm pretty tired."

"So am I," Clint said. "Good-night."

"'night, and thanks for everything you've done, and everythin' you're gonna do."

"I'm just going to keep you alive, Carl," Clint said. "You're going to do the rest."

Wainwright closed his door and Clint walked down the hall to his own room. He stopped in front of the door; there was no indication that anyone was waiting for him inside. There were times when he felt it, and he was usually right, there was either a woman in his bed or a man with a gun waiting for him.

He opened the door, his hand hovering near his gun, just in case. But the room was empty, with no sign that anyone was ever there, except him.

He lit the lamp on the wall by the door and turned it up high, then walked to the bed. He removed his gun belt and hung on the bedpost. Then he sat and pulled off his boots. His saddlebags were on the bed so he dragged one over and took out the book he was currently reading, a collection called *The Raven and Other Poems*.

He set the book down on the small table next to the bed, then swung his legs up onto the bed and sat with his back against the bed rail. He reached for the book and started reading, rather than think about what the next day might bring . . .

***

He had read for half an hour when a knock came at the door. Once again, he thought it would either be a woman or a man with a gun. If it was a woman, it was probably Gina, the only one he'd met in town, so far. As for a man with a gun, it could be any of the bushwhackers. But it was most likely the hangman, Wainwright. He was probably hearing sounds in the hall, again.

Whoever it was, he slipped his gun from the hanging holster and took it with him to the door.

"Who is it?"

"A friend." It was a woman's voice, but he couldn't tell if it was Gina. "Let me in, please, before somebody comes along."

He opened the door and looked at her. It wasn't Gina, but the other saloon girl, Rusty.

"Come on in."

She entered, and he closed the door.

"Are we friends?" he asked, walking to the bedpost and holstering the gun.

"We could be." She smiled, still wearing her make-up and dress from the saloon. He hadn't had a good look at her while talking to Gina. It would have been rude. She was older than the other girl, probably in her 30s, well-built and pretty. As a younger girl, maybe ten years ago, she was probably beautiful, but she'd been at her job for too long.

"Is that why you're here?" he asked. "To make friends?"

"Gina said you weren't interested in payin'."

"I'm not."

"Well, she told me she was gonna come up here and give it away."

"And?"

She shrugged.

"I thought I'd beat her to it."

"Why?"

"You're the Gunsmith," she said. "That's what they're sayin'. And I've been at the game longer than Gina has. I figure you need a gal with experience."

"Are you and Gina competitors?" he asked.

"Once in a while," she admitted. She moved closer to him.

"But what does it matter? Couldn't you use a little comfort, tonight?"

He studied her, breathed her in, enjoyed how the gown showed off her pale, smooth shoulders.

"Just a little comfort," she said, lowering her voice, "free of charge."

He reached out and touched her shoulder. She closed her eyes as he ran his fingertips over her skin.

"Tell me something," he said.

"What's that?"

"Why Rusty?" he said. "I'd expect somebody by that name to have red hair."

"I got it when I was a kid," she told him. "My hair was kinda rust colored back then, but as I got older it turned blonde."

"Ah," he said, trailing his fingers down her chest to her cleavage, and then the flat of his hand down over her belly. "Everywhere?"

She shrugged, which made her breasts jiggle nicely.

"There might still be some rust . . . somewhere," she admitted.

She reached behind her to undo the stays of her dress, making it fall to the floor.

Chapter Ten

Clint had experienced the intense heat that a woman's body can give off many times before. But Rusty's bountiful flesh seemed to be filling the entire room with its sultriness.

She unbuttoned his shirt, slid her hands inside, tilted her head up and kissed him. The kiss became avid and she slid the shirt completely off him and tossed it aside. Next, she started on his trousers and he decided to cooperate to get as naked as she was as soon as possible.

When his pants came off her eyes and hands went to his burgeoning cock. She went to her knees, began to stroke it and coo to it, slid one hand beneath his testicles to fondle them.

"My God . . ." she said, breathlessly. "We should go to bed so I can give this the attention it deserves."

"I was thinking the same thing," he said.

They moved to the bed together, then split to go to either side. After pulling the sheets down they came together in the center of it, their bodies pressed together as they kissed again.

"Get on your back," she whispered to him. "I'm gonna enjoy you."

"I think I'm going to enjoy you first," he said. She shrieked and laughed as he flipped her onto her back.

Clint relished roaming a woman's body with his hands, his mouth, his tongue. He kissed her neck, her shoulders, her big breasts and nipples. She sighed as he lingered there, biting them, worrying them between his teeth while he flicked them with his tongue. Then he continued to work down further, kissing her tummy, her belly button, working down to her smooth thighs, enjoying the scent that was coming from her vagina, showing how ready she was.

He laid down between her legs, still kissing her thighs, reaching up to fondle her breasts, and then pressing his face to her wetness. As he started to lick her she gasped, reached down and grasped his head.

She wet his face with her nectar, in a series of eruptions before she spasmed violently and began to bounce on the bed. He tried to keep his mouth in contact with her, but finally had to pull away and let her ride out her pleasure as it coursed through her body.

"Jesus!" she gasped. "Ain't no man ever done that to me before."

"That's because you don't spend enough time," he said, sliding his hands up and down her thighs.

"You're right," she said, still trying to catch her breath. "They ain't worth nothin' but a quick poke."

"That's what they pay for, isn't it?" he asked.

"Yeah, it is."

"And they don't worry about what you get out of it."

Her eyes brightened.

"So this is why you don't pay for sex," she said. "You don't have to, when you can do this to a woman."

He moved up and laid down next to her, on his back. He kept his left hand on her right thigh. With his right he would have been able to reach his gun in a split second, if he had to.

Her hand strayed over and began to stoke his hard cock, again.

"Now you need some attention," she said, "some lovin'."

"Why don't you relax—"

"Huh-uh," she said, rolling over and siding down so she was between his legs. "Let me show you what you get when I do take my time, when I'm in it for more than just a quick poke."

She took him in both her hands, pressed him to her face, her cheeks, nuzzled him, then opened her mouth and took him inside.

Clint gasped as Rusty took the entire length of him in. Her heat closed around him and then she began to bob up and down on him. The sucking was gentle at first, but then it became more avid as she moved faster and faster.

Just as he thought he couldn't hold out any longer she released him from her mouth, gasping for air as she smiled up at him.

"More?" she asked.

"Much more," he said.

"Can you last?"

"As long as you can."

"Good," she said, and bent to her task, again.

The amount of pleasure she proceeded to give him moved into the realm of pain—beautiful pain. She slid her hands beneath him to cup his bottom, and seemed to be able to take him even deeper that way. There were times when he thought she might choke, but she just kept going, and he kept holding out, holding on as long as he could until, finally, with a long, guttural moan he let go and exploded. She took it all, continuing to suck him until he was empty, or thought he was, because then she seemed to be able to draw even more from him. Just when he thought the pleasure/pain was going to be too much for him, she released him and, laughing, laid down next to him to catch her breath.

"Let's see if Gina," she said, a bit later, "can match that."

Chapter Eleven

Rusty didn't stay.

"If I do," she said, "we'll go at it again, and it'll kill one of us—probably you. But maybe me."

He watched her put her dress back on, and then she blew him a kiss and went out the door. He desperately hoped that Gina wouldn't show up, because he never would have been able to accommodate her. He was worn out, and ready to sleep . . .

***

Gratefully, no one else knocked on his door that night, not Gina, and not Wainwright.

When he woke he had the smell of Rusty all over him. He wanted a bath, but thought he should tell Wainwright so that the man wouldn't be looking for him.

When he knocked on the hangman's door the man answered right away. He was still wearing the same shirt and trousers he'd had on the day before, but his feet were bare. His hair was flying in all directions.

"How was your night?" Clint asked.

"Fitful."

"I'm going to take a bath this morning, and then we can have breakfast. How's that?"

"Suits me."

J.R. Roberts

"I'll knock on your door again."

"Right."

He closed the door and Clint went downstairs to arrange for the bath.

***

The Fate Inn had a small, well-appointed dining room. Clint was able to get a table up against a side wall, away from windows or the doorway.

He felt refreshed from the bath, and there was only the hint of Rusty in his nostrils, which suited him. Wainwright had put on a fresh shirt, and he had combed his hair.

When the waiter came they ordered coffee and ham-and-eggs, each.

"What's first today?" Clint asked, while they were eating.

"I have to weigh and measure the prisoner," Wainwright said. "Then I'll have to examine the gallows. After that it's all about the rope."

"I see."

"It has to be the right length, the right thickness, the right strength," Wainwright said. "Nothing can go wrong. I have to make sure the man's neck snaps immediately, or else it could be . . . inhumane."

"I get it."

But Wainwright went on.

"I know people like it when a man is dancing on the end of a rope because his neck didn't break. They like to watch a man be strangled as he hangs there. I don't. It's my job to see that doesn't happen."

"And here I thought the hangman's job was just to kill him," Clint said.

"There's a lot more to it than that," Wainwright said. "Come on, I'll show ya rather than just tell ya."

They paid for their breakfast and left the hotel.

***

They went directly to the sheriff's office, where Sheriff Hastings was not surprised to see them.

"'mornin', gents," he said. I've been expectin' you."

"Sheriff," Wainwright said, "I'll need to see the prisoner right away."

"Of course," Hastings said. "Mr. Adams, too?"

"Yes," Wainwright said, "I'm keepin' him with me, everywhere."

"I don't blame you." Hastings looked at Clint. "I still don't know anythin' about who ambushed Mr. Wainwright."

"I hope you'll keep looking," Clint said.

"I will."

He grabbed a key ring off the wall and showed them to the cell block, which had two cells. Only one was occupied at the moment. Clint assumed it was Dave Miklin.

"Company, Dave," the sheriff said.

"I don't want no damn company," the young man in the cell said.

"Sorry," Hastings said, "you got no choice."

J.R. Roberts

He was lying on his back, so he turned his head to look at them.

"Who are they?"

"This is your hangman," Hastings said, "Mister—"

"No names," Wainwright said, "Please."

"Fine," Hastings said. "This is your hangman, and this fella here is Clint Adams."

Miklin sat up.

"The Gunsmith?"

"That's right," Hastings said.

"What's he doin' here?" Miklin asked. "Are you gonna shoot me? Is that it?"

"He's with me," Wainwright said, taking out a tape measure. "I'll need to measure you."

"I thought you wanted to weigh him, too," the sheriff commented.

"Yes," Wainwright said, "my scale is in the back of my wagon. I'll bring it over later."

"Suit yerself," Hastings said, unlocking the cell. "Go ahead."

Miklin stood up and said, "If he comes in here I'll—"

"You'll what?" Clint asked. "Kill him?"

"I ain't no killer!" Miklin snapped. "I told the judge that."

"Well then, you won't kill anybody here, will you?" Clint asked. "So just stand nice and still and let the man do his job."

"So he can hang me?"

"So he can do it properly," Clint said. "Do you want to dance at the end of the rope, strangling while the people cheer?"

42

"No."

"Then stand still, Dave."

Wainwright entered the cell and measured Miklin while the young man withstood it.

"Thank you," Wainwright said to him, leaving the cell.

Hastings locked it up again.

"Thank you," Wainwright said again, this time to the sheriff.

"Sure."

They left the cell block.

"I'll be back later with my scale," Wainwright said.

He and Clint left the office.

Chapter Twelve

Just outside, on the boardwalk, Clint asked, "Why didn't we bring the scale with us this time?"

"It's a game I play with myself," Wainwright said. "I measure the man, then try to guess his weight."

"What's your guess?"

"He's six foot one," the hangman said. "I'm guessing . . . oh, one seventy-six."

"That precise?"

"Yes."

"Well," Clint asked, "what's next?"

"Let's take a look at the gallows."

***

Clint watched while Wainwright first walked around the structure, alternately, testing its strength with a kick, or by leaning on it. Then he went up the stairs and walked around on top of it, doing the same.

"What's he doin'?"

Clint turned to see the man who had spoken. He was in his 40s, wearing work clothes, the sleeves of his shirt rolled up to exhibit very large forearms.

"He's testing it to make sure it's secure," Clint said.

"He the hangman?" the man asked.

"He is. Who are you?"

"I'm the carpenter," the man said. "Me and my men built it."

"It looks pretty good to me," Clint said.

"Thanks. What does he think?"

"I don't know, yet. Why don't you wait for him to come down and ask him yourself?"

"Sure."

They both watched while Wainwright completed his examination, and then came down the stairs.

"Carl, this is the man who built the gallows," Clint said, "uh . . ."

"Jerry Corston."

They shook hands.

"What d'ya think?" Corston asked.

"You did a fine job," Wainwright said. "It's very solid and secure."

"Thanks. I pride myself on my work. This is actually the second one we did."

"Second?" Clint asked. "What happened to the first?"

"It burned down."

"Was it burned deliberately?" Clint asked.

"Oh, yeah," Corston said. "Not everybody in town agrees with this hangin'."

"Do you?"

"It don't matter to me," Corston said. "It's just my job to build it."

"Do you know who burned it?" Clint asked.

"Not a clue," the man said.

"Guess," Clint said.

Corston frowned.

"Who are you? Another hangman? I didn't think they'd send two."

"My name's Clint Adams," Clint said. "Somebody tried to ambush this man yesterday. Tried to kill him. I'd like to find out who they were. Now I'm thinking maybe they were the same ones who burned down your gallows."

"Oh well," Corston said, "if I had to guess, I'd say it was somebody who works for the old man."

"Old man?"

"Miklin's old man," Corston clarified. "He said in court he wasn't about to stand by and watch his son hang. Not if he could do something about it."

"And has he done anything about it?"

"Not that I know of," Corston said, "but maybe his men have tried, d'ya think? Twice?"

Chapter Thirteen

"You want to do what?" Wainwright asked.

"Talk to Dave Miklin's father."

"Where?"

"I assume I'll have to ride out to his ranch to see him," Clint said.

They had walked from the gallows to the stable where they had boarded their horses and Wainwright's wagon.

"And what should I do while you're doin' that?" the hangman asked.

"You have two options, that I can see," Clint said. "Barricade yourself in your room or come with me."

"Go with you? To see the man whose son I am to hang?" Wainwright asked.

"To find out if he's the one who sent those men to ambush you," Clint said.

"Do you think he'll admit it?"

"Face-to-face, maybe he will," Clint said. "After all, he did let it be known that he wasn't just going to sit back and let his son hang."

"When would you want to do this?" Wainwright asked.

"I don't know—now? It's still early."

"How far away is the ranch?"

"I don't know how far it is, or where it is," Clint admitted. "Why don't we find out?"

"Whatever you say," Wainwright responded. "You're keepin' me alive, so I'm stayin' with you."

***

They found the livery man and got the answers to their questions. The Miklin ranch—called the Bar-MK—was south of town about an hour or so.

"It's an easy ride," the man said. "Just stay on the road. Ya can't miss it."

Clint rented a horse for Wainwright, they saddled their two horses, and left the livery. They didn't bother telling the sheriff where they were going. Clint didn't want to take a chance on word getting to Henry Miklin first.

***

Their directions were correct. They stayed on the road and eventually came to a metal archway that had BAR-MK RANCH written on it. They rode underneath it and followed the road to a two-story ranch house, with a large barn and corral across from it. Clint had ridden into many ranches in the past, and the arrival of a stranger—or two—was always an occasion to stop work and look. This was no different. The ranch hands who were working in the corral, and the ones who were watching, all stopped to see who was riding in.

"What if that's them?" Wainwright asked, looking over at the collection of men. "The bushwhackers."

"Those are ranch hands," Clint told him, but he was thinking the same thing. "I guess we'll find out, though."

For the time being he didn't feel threatened by the men because the ones he could see clearly weren't armed.

One of the men broke off from the rest, and walked with authority toward Clint and Wainwright. Clint assumed he was either top hand, or the foreman. In his late 30s, he looked too young to be Henry Miklin.

"Can I help ya?" he asked.

"Looking for Mr. Miklin," Clint said.

"What's it about?"

"His son."

"His son is about to hang," the man said.

"I know, that's why I thought he might talk to me."

"I'm the foreman of this ranch, Bill Cameron. Mr. Miklin ain't here, he's out lookin' at some fence damage we heard about west of here."

"We could ride out there and see him, if you'd give us directions."

The man frowned.

"Mister, you ain't law from what I can see."

"No, I'm not," Clint admitted. "I'm just a good citizen who wants to talk to Mr. Miklin about his son.

"A good citizen with a name?"

Clint nodded. "Clint Adams."

Cameron looked dubious.

"Yer kiddin'."

"I'm not."

"Prove it."

49

Clint looked over at the ranch hands who were watching, some of them still perched on the corral fence.

"You want me to shoot one of those fellas off the fence from here?" Clint asked. "Which one?"

"No, no," Cameron said, "don't shoot nobody. If that's who you say you are . . . who would make a target out of himself by takin' your name?"

"Good point," Clint said. "Mr. Miklin?"

Chapter Fourteen

Clint and Wainwright followed the foreman's directions and finally saw four riders up ahead of them, sitting on horses along a fence line. As they got closer Clint could see that part of the fence had either fallen over, or been knocked down.

Then, as Clint and the hangman approached, the riders noticed them and turned to face them.

"Can I help you with something?" an older man asked them.

"You can if you're Henry Miklin."

"I am," Miklin said, "and who are you?"

"My name's Clint Adams, Mr. Miklin," Clint said. "This man is Carlton Wainwright—he's the hangman who's here because of your son."

"Because of the judge, you mean," Miklin said. His attitude was not quite what Clint had been expecting, especially once he introduced Wainwright. "What do you want?"

"Just to talk," Clint said.

"I'm busy."

"It won't take long."

Miklin studied them, then turned to his three men.

"Keep riding further along, see what you can find," he told them.

Are you sure, Mr. Miklin?" one of them asked.

"I'll be fine, Joe," Miklin said. "I don't think the Gunsmith is here to kill me. Just do it."

"Yessir."

The three riders started off, with the one called Joe constantly looking over his shoulder.

"You're *not* here to kill me, are you?" Miklin asked.

"No, sir," Clint said, "that's not my intention."

"Then what's on your mind, Adams?" Miklin asked. "Why would you bring the man who is to kill my son out here to see me?"

"To ask if you've tried to kill him," Clint said.

"What?"

"Or if you had your men burn down the gallows in town," Clint added.

Miklin frowned.

"I suspect that some of my hands got liquored up and may have burned that gallows down," Miklin admitted. "I don't hold it against them. In their drunken state they may have thought they were being loyal. That's even if they did do it. But what's this about trying to kill this man?" Miklin looked at the hangman. "What's your name? Wainwright?"

"That's right, sir," Wainwright said. "I was ambushed yesterday by about five men, who tried to kill me. If Mr. Adams hadn't come along when he did, I'd be dead."

"Is that something else your men would do out of loyalty, Mr. Miklin?" Clint asked.

"It better not be!" Miklin roared. "I'll have their heads."

"Isn't it true you said in court that your son wouldn't hang if you could help it?" Clint asked.

"I meant legally," Miklin said. "I meant that I would prove he didn't do it. Not that I'd kill the hangman. Good God, man, another one would just be sent. I wouldn't be able to kill them all, would I?"

"My thinking exactly," Clint said.

"Then why are you here?"

"I thought I'd take the direct approach to find out, and ask you."

"Well, you've asked, man," Miklin said.

"Yes, I have," Clint said. "What's more, I believe you."

Miklin looked at the hangman.

"Wainwright, I hold no malice toward you. I know you'll just be doing your job."

"Thank you, Mr. Miklin."

"But somebody's trying to stop him," Clint said. "Any idea who that could be? Do you have another son?"

"I do not," Miklin said. "Dave is my only boy. And I have a daughter."

"A daughter," Clint said. "And how does she feel about this whole thing?"

"She's devastated, to say the least," Miklin said.

"Would she recruit any of your hands for this kind of a job?" Clint asked.

"She couldn't—she wouldn't—" Miklin blustered, and then stopped. "I tell you what, Mr. Adams. I'd like you and Wainwright, here, to ride back to my house with me. Let's ask her."

"Well, I didn't mean—" Clint started. "I mean, a young woman wouldn't—"

"No, no," Miklin said, cutting him off. "You employed the direct approach with me, let's do the same with Belinda. Will you do it?"

Clint exchanged a look with Wainwright, which told him the hangman was leaving the decision up to him.

"Well, sure," Clint said. "But what about your men—"

"They'll be checking the fences for hours," Miklin said. "And after that they'll figure out that I went back to the house."

"All right."

"And while we're there we can have a drink," the rancher said. "I have a proposition for you."

Clint wondered, as they rode back, if the proposition would be an offer for him to kill the hangman? No, he thought the man was telling the truth. It would have to be something else. But what?

Chapter Fifteen

Since they came riding back with the boss, Clint and Wainwright didn't attract as much attention as they had the first time. Still, the foreman came over to see what was going on.

"Anythin' I can do, boss?" he asked.

"It's okay, Bill," Miklin said. "These gentlemen are here at my invitation."

"Shall I take the horses, then?"

"Yes, see to them, unsaddle mine, but have these gent's horses ready to them at a moment's notice."

"Yessir."

As they dismounted and handed their reins to the foreman Miklin said to Clint, "That's a fine animal. You wouldn't be interested in selling him, would you?"

"Not a chance," Clint said.

"I didn't think so. Well come, inside."

Clint and Wainwright followed Miklin up the stairs and into the house.

"My daughter's around here somewhere," he said. "I'll find her. Why don't you both wait for me in there." He pointed to a well-furnished living room.

"All right," Clint said.

As they entered the room and Miklin disappeared into the house Wainwright asked Clint, "You don't think this could be a trap, do you?"

"I doubt it," Clint said. "Not in his own house. Besides, like I said before, I believe him."

"Yeah, but what about the daughter?"

"We're about to find out," Clint said, as they heard footsteps coming back.

Clint didn't know he had expected when Miklin said he had a daughter, but it wasn't the beautiful woman who walked into the room. She was tall, blonde, in her 20s, looking very self- assured, her long hair hanging down over her shoulders. The dress she wore told him that she enjoyed showing off her body to the men on the ranch. Could she have used that body to convince some men to ambush Wainwright, keep him from getting to town? Or had she simply used money? Or both?

"Gentleman," Miklin said, "my daughter, Belinda. My dear, Clint Adams and Mr. Carlton Wainwright."

Belinda gave Clint a glance, then set her sights on Wainwright.

"So you're the man who's going to hang my idiot brother?" she asked.

"I, uh, yes, I suppose I am."

"Idiot?" Clint asked.

"What else would you call him?" she demanded, looking at Clint with her eyes flashing. "Killing another boy over a girl? Idiot's the only word I can think of."

"Now, Belinda, that's enough," Miklin said. "Your brother's not an idiot—"

"No, of course not," she said. "He's the genius who's going to take over your business when you're gone. Or maybe

56

not, if this man does his job. Then maybe you'll leave it to me, your first born."

"That's enough!" he said to her "If you're not going to be civil you might as well leave us."

"With pleasure." She turned and stormed out.

"Well, there you have it," Miklin said. "She'll be very happy when you hang my son, because that will leave her as the only heir. So do you still think she might have sent some men to ambush Mr. Wainwright?"

Clint studied the man. He and his daughter could have worked up that little act before they came into the room. But the look in the young woman's eyes had looked real, to Clint, who considered himself a good judge of character.

"No," Clint said, "I don't."

Miklin walked to a small sideboard with some decanters on it. He poured three tumblers of something and brought them over to Clint and Wainwright.

"Brandy," he said. "Or would you prefer whiskey?"

Clint didn't prefer either, so he said, "This is fine."

"Thank you," Wainwright said. He sniffed it before he drank. Clint wondered if he was thinking it might be poisoned?

"She's right, of course," Miklin said.

"About what?" Clint asked.

"My son," the man said. "He's an idiot, but he's the only son I've got. I thought he'd run the place when I was gone, with Belinda's help, of course. She's got a head for the business."

"Then why not just leave it her?" Clint asked.

"It's probably a moot point, now," he said. "I'll have to leave it to her after Dave is . . . gone." He shook his head. "Parents shouldn't outlive their children."

"I agree," Clint said.

"Then maybe you'll help me, Adams," Miklin said.

"How?"

"Prove my son innocent," the rancher said. "I tried getting Pinkertons here to do it, but they'd never be in time. The same for Talbot Roper, in Denver. But you, you're here already."

"What makes you think—"

"I know about you," Miklin said. "I know your reputation is as a gunman, but I also know there's more to you."

"How do you know that?"

"I read newspapers, And I investigated you once."

"Oh? Why?"

"I was thinking of hiring you for a job I needed done."

"What happened?"

"Once I realized you were more than just a mindless gunman, I went another way."

"I see."

"I found myself a truly mindless gunman," Miklin added. "But for this I need someone with a brain. That'd be you."

"Well, I'm not a detective—"

"I'll pay you a thousand dollars to prove he didn't do it," Miklin said, cutting him off.

Clint looked at Wainwright, who was sipping his brandy and listening.

"What if I find out he did it?" Clint asked.

"I'll still pay you."

"I don't have very much time," Clint said. "He's due to be hanged tomorrow."

Miklin looked at Wainwright.

"Couldn't you do something about that?"

"Well," the hangman said, "I've measured him, inspected the gallows . . . I haven't weighed him, yet."

"Couldn't something go wrong with your scale?" Miklin asked.

Clint looked at Wainwright and raised his eyebrows.

"Well . . ." the hangman said.

Chapter Sixteen

Clint and Wainwright discussed the matter as they rode back.

"I don't know if this is right," the hangman said.

"What's that?"

"My claiming that my scale is off, so that we can extend the prisoner's life a day or two."

"Just to give me time to ask a few questions," Clint reminded him. "To see if he's really guilty."

"Yes, but I shouldn't be concerned with that," Wainwright said. "A judge found him guilty and sentenced him to hang. I should just do my job."

"A job you're not sure you even want to do, anymore," Clint said. "What if this gives you time to really give it some thought?"

"Yeah, I suppose you're right," the man said.

"And if the boy does die, what's the difference if it's in a day or two?"

"I suppose," Wainwright said. "I've just never thought about it that way before."

"So if you weren't the hangman," Clint asked, "what would you think?"

"About what, exactly?"

"Miklin, his daughter—"

"They have some problems, don't they?" the hangman said. "A girl who hopes her brother dies because he's an idiot and would inherit the ranch."

"Yeah, that's a problem, all right."

"And she hates her father."

Surprised, Clint asked, "Why do you say that?"

"The look on her face," he said. "I've seen many expressions like that, over the years. People watching someone they hated hang, and all."

"I didn't notice that."

"It's one thing I can do," Wainwright said. "Other than hang people. Read faces."

"You know," Clint said, "if I'm going to look into this, I should talk to her."

"Do you wanna go back?"

"No," Clint said, "I'll start in town, as soon as we get back. We can stop in at the sheriff's first and tell him the lie about the scale."

"I'm a terrible liar," Wainwright admitted.

"Then I suppose you better never get married," Clint said. "That is, if you're not already married?"

"No, I'm not."

"Well," Clint said, "suppose I explain it to the sheriff. As it happens I'm a damned good liar."

Chapter Seventeen

"What's wrong with the damned thing?" Sheriff Hastings asked Clint.

"I don't know," Clint said. "It's not working properly."

"Can't use another scale?" Hastings asked. "The one at the feed store, for example?"

"No," Clint said, "according to Mr. Wainwright it has to be his official scale."

"So what do we do now?" the sheriff demanded. "Can he take it to somebody in town to repair it?"

"No," Clint said, "he and I are going to fix it, but it may take an extra day."

"You're gonna fix it?" Hastings said. "What do you know about scales?"

"Gunsmith is not only my reputation," Clint said, "it's what I do. I should be able to figure out a scale. So you better tell whoever you need to that the hanging will be moved by a day, maybe two."

Hastings frowned.

"I'll have to tell the mayor," he said, "and the editor of the newspaper."

"This town has a newspaper?"

"Small town," the sheriff said, "small newspaper."

"Well," Clint said, "I suggest you do what you have to do, and we'll get to work."

"Where's the hangman right now?" Hastings asked.

"He's working on the scale," Clint said. "I'm going to go and help him."

"Well," the lawman said, sourly, "let me know when it's fixed."

"I will."

Clint left the office, didn't go to the stable where the wagon and scale were, but to his hotel, where he found Wainwright barricaded in his room. After he knocked he heard the man remove the chair from beneath the doorknob.

"Did he believe it?" the man asked, as Clint entered.

"He believed it."

"So what do we do now?"

"Well," Clint said, "technically, you and me are in the barn, trying to fix the scale."

"So if he goes there and doesn't find us . . ."

". . . we'll have to come up with a reason why."

"And what would that be?" Wainwright asked.

"We could tell him that we need a part," Clint said. "How big is the scale? Can we bring it here?"

"It's heavy," Wainwright said. "I'll be taking my wagon over to the sheriff's office in order to weigh the prisoner."

"Okay," Clint said, "are there some parts that we could bring up here?"

"Yes!" Wainwright said, brightening. "We could do that."

"And you can stay in the room while I'm out asking questions."

"What about when the sheriff hears that you've been doin' that?"

"We'll deal with that when the time comes. Right now let's go over and grab some parts."

***

At the stable they were watched by the livery man, who didn't seem to have anything else to do, so they made a show of removing a couple of parts from the scale, examining them, and then taking them along when they left. If the sheriff asked the man what he saw, no damage done.

Clint escorted Wainwright back to his hotel room, and waited in the hall until he heard the man shove a wooden chairback beneath the doorknob, before leaving.

Clint made a stop at the hardware store to ask the man if he had any of the parts they needed for the scale. Wainwright gave him the name of a few pieces he knew a regular hardware store would not stock. This was just for the benefit of the sheriff, if he happened to stop and ask if they had come by.

But he did find out something helpful while he was there. The owner of the hardware store, whose named was Bill Riggs, told him that he had been on the jury that found Dave Miklin guilty.

"Is that so?" Clint asked.

"Yeah," the 50ish, beefy man said, "the kid was grinning 'cause he thought he was gonna get off 'cause of who his daddy was."

"Not so, huh?"

"Naw," Riggs said. "if anythin' I think it hurt him."

"How's that?"

"There were a few people on the jury who didn't care if old man Miklin pulled out of town."

"So there were some who did care, huh?" Clint asked.

"Oh yeah," Riggs said, "out of twelve probably more than half of 'em got businesses here."

"Like you, huh?"

"Me? That didn't have nothin' to do with my decision," Riggs assured him. "I went by the evidence."

"So you were a good juror huh?"

"I sure was."

"Who were some of the other good jurors?"

Riggs was not only happy to give him those names, but the names of both lawyers in the case, as well.

Clint thanked the man for his help and left.

Chapter Eighteen

The prosecuting attorney—like the judge—was not in town. He had been called in to work the case. But the attorney who defended the boy was a resident. In fact, he was Henry Miklin's regular lawyer.

"I handle all of Mr. Miklin's business," Alan Cunningham told Clint, "criminal or otherwise."

"Everything?"

"Everything," the man assured him. "Why else would I be living in this one-horse town." The man, in his 30s, had an office on the main street, but it was small and over a dress shop. He clearly wasn't happy with his lot in life. "Maybe that's one good thing that will come out of this, though."

"What's that?"

"If Dave hangs, Henry will pull all his business out of this town," Cunningham said. "That means I'll be able to leave and live in a real town."

Clint wondered if Alan Cunningham's desire to leave the town of Fate might have influenced the man's performance as a defense attorney?

"Can I ask you, do you think he did it?" Clint asked.

Cunningham regarded Clint across his desk.

"You say you're working for the old man?"

"That's right."

"I'm going to be checking with him, you know."

"Do it," Clint said. "He offered me a thousand dollars to prove whether his son did it, or not."

"*Did* it or not?" Cunningham asked. "He didn't tell you to prove he didn't do it?"

"I told him I'd try, but I might end up proving he did kill the other boy. He said he'd pay me anyway."

"Well, well," Cunningham said, "I'm going to have to raise my rates."

"Do you think he did it?"

"He's stupid enough to have done it," the lawyer said. "I just don't think he has the nerve to kill anybody."

"Who was the girl they were fighting over?"

"Pretty little thing named Evelyn Hargrove."

"Miklin and the boy he killed, they both thought she was their girlfriend? What did she say?"

"She didn't testify."

"Why not?"

"The judge said she didn't have to."

"Again, why not?"

"You'd have to ask him," Cunningham said.

"What's his name?"

"Judge Bennett," the lawyer said.

"And where is he now?"

"He's on the circuit," Cunningham said. "He should be coming back here in about . . . three months."

"Well," Clint said, standing, "I can't stay here that long, and the kid's going to hang in a day or two."

"Tomorrow, isn't it?"

"Not anymore," Clint said, and explained why.

"You're kidding."

"I'm not."

"Miklin's money buys a lot."

"Well, it's not going to buy the boy off, not if he did it," Clint said. He went to the door, stopped and turned. "Thanks for talking to me. I may want to talk to you again."

"I'll be here."

***

Clint's next stop was the Lodge Saloon. It wasn't busy that early in the evening, but both Gina and Rusty were there, at the end of the bar. As Clint entered, the two girls said something to each other. This time it was Rusty who came down the bar toward him, and Gina who stayed behind, looked decidedly unhappy. It was obvious Rusty had told the younger girl about her visit to his room.

"Lookin' for me?" Rusty asked. She was wearing another shoulder baring dress.

"Actually, I'm looking for Gina," Clint said.

"What?" Rusty said. "But I thought—"

"I just need to talk to her, Rusty."

"Can't you talk to me?"

"Not about Dave Miklin."

"Oh, that!" Rusty said. "Yeah, she was involved in that. Ain't you helpin' the man who's gonna hang 'im?"

"Yes, I am," Clint said, "that's why I need to talk to her. I need to make sure Miklin is guilty before he's hanged."

"Well, I'll tell 'er," Rusty said, "but you just make sure all you do is talk."

"We can do it right here, at a table," he offered.

"That's fine."

Chapter Nineteen

Gina sat at a back table with Clint, still looking unhappy.

"So, you wanna tell me why you went with Rusty and you didn't go with me?"

"I didn't go with Rusty, Gina," Clint sad. "She came to me. And no money changed hands."

"Really?" She looked shocked. "She gave you a free poke?"

"Oh, yes," Clint said. "But that's not what I'm here to talk about. I want to talk about Dave Miklin and Evelyn Hargrove."

She looked puzzled. "Why?"

"Because he's going to hang for a murder he committed fighting over her."

"Hey," she said, "she didn't have nothin' to do with him, or with that other feller, what's his name."

"You don't remember it?"

"I never knew his name," she said. "Them two came in here, started to talk to me and then started fighting with each other. I heard Evelyn's name once, but I don't know why."

Listening to her, Clint realized he didn't know the victim's name, either.

"So neither of those fellas was her boyfriend," he asked.

"She's sixteen years old. She should have boyfriends, but her dad won't let her."

Clint was beginning to understand why Evelyn never testi-
fied. She had nothing to contribute, and saying what he'd just
heard in court would have confused the issue.

"Well, okay, then," Clint said. "If that's true, then I don't
need to bother you about this."

"I gotta get to work," she said, and left the table.

Clint decided that he had to go right to the horse's mouth
about this whole thing.

***

"You wanna what?" Sheriff Hastings said.

"I want to talk to Dave Miklin," Clint said. "Is there a
problem with that?"

"What's that got to do with weighin' him?" Hastings
asked.

"Nothing," Clint said. "Wainwright is working on the scale
right now. This is something else, entirely."

"You mind if I ask what?"

"Wainwright is a hangman," Clint said. "He doesn't want
to get to know his subject. I do, though. I want to talk to the
young man. I promise I won't try to break him out."

Hastings just shrugged his shoulders and said, "Yeah,
okay. Come on."

He grabbed the key and led Clint into the cell block.

"Hey, kid," he said to Miklin, "the Gunsmith wants to talk
to you. I don't know why, but here he is." He looked at Clint.
"I ain't openin' the cell door, so I'll just take this key back out
with me."

71

"That's fine," Clint said. "I don't need the door open."

Hastings left, closing the cell block door behind him.

Dave Miklin did not move from his supine position on the cot.

"Your daddy sent me, Dave."

"What?" The boy looked at Clint, then sat up. "You gonna break me out?"

"No," Clint said, "that's not why I'm here."

"Then why *are* you here?"

"He wants me to find out whether or not you committed this murder."

"You mean he wants you to prove I didn't do it."

"Did you?"

"Hell, no! I told my Pa that, I told the sheriff that, I told the jury and I told the judge. And now I'm tellin' you. I didn't kill Roy Tillman."

"Did you know this Tillman?"

"Well, sure, I knew 'im. I know lots of people in town."

"What about the girl, Evelyn?"

"She's a kid," Miklin said. "That's all I know."

"Then tell me what happened."

"I told everybody," Miklin said. "I was havin' a drink in the Lodge when Tillman came in, stood beside me, ordered a beer and then started sayin' stuff about Evelyn Hargrove, and me and my father under his breath—but so people could hear, ya know?"

"And then what?"

"I told him to shut his mouth. He came at me and I punched him. He said I'd be sorry, and ran out. Two hours later I'm gettin' arrested for killin' him!"

"Had you left the saloon?"

"I was on my way to my horse when the sheriff got the drop on me."

"Were you armed?"

"Well, yeah, I don't come to town unarmed. There's too many people got it in for my pa. They'd take it out on me, if they could. Hell, that's what they're doin' now!"

The boy had worked his way to the front of the cell, and now had his hands wrapped around the bar.

"Mr. Adams, if my pa sent you to help me, you gotta get me outta here." He lowered his voice. "The sheriff ain't no match for you."

"I'm not breaking you out, Dave," Clint said. "If I get you out it'll be legal."

"B-but . . . they're hangin' me tomorrow."

"Don't be too sure of that," Clint said. "I'll talk to you again."

Chapter Twenty

"Sheriff," Clint said, coming out of the cell block, "why did you arrest him?"

"What?" Hastings looked up from his desk. "What're you talkin' about?"

"I was just wondering what it was that made you arrest him?" Clint asked.

"He's a killer."

"Yeah, but how did you know that when you arrested him?" Clint asked.

Hastings sat back in his chair.

"I did my job, Adams," Hastings said. "I determined that Dave killed Tillman, and I arrested him. A judge and a jury agreed with me. I don't need to explain myself to you."

"Have you explained it to Henry Miklin?"

"I told Mr. Miklin that I arrested his son, and what for," Hastings said. "And I told him that he'd better get the boy a lawyer. After that Miklin's lawyer talked to the prosecutor."

"Weren't you afraid of what Henry Miklin would do?"

Hastings shook his head.

"He's a powerful rancher," the lawman said, "but he doesn't break the law. No, I wasn't worried. Everything was done legally."

"Was anyone worried about what he'd do?" Clint asked. "I mean, after what he said at the trial?"

"Well, sure," Hastings said. "I think I told you before, lots of people were worried that he'd pull out of town. The mayor was real worried that the arrest would kill this town."

"The arrest would kill the town," Clint repeated.

"Well, yeah."

"Not the murder itself?"

"Look, I just meant—"

"And not Miklin pulling out," Clint said, "but the arrest. Did the mayor blame you for that?"

"He probably did," Hastings said, "but what else was I supposed to do? It's my job, what he pays me for."

"And did he finally understand that?"

Hastings made a face. "Not really. I think he's waitin' to see how this all plays out."

"I see."

"If you wanna know how he feels, you should talk to him," the lawman suggested.

"I probably will."

"What's goin' on?" Hastings asked. "I thought you were just bodyguarding the hangman."

"I was," Clint said, "but I've been asked to look into the murder."

"By who?"

"Henry Miklin."

Hastings raised his eyebrows. "So you're a detective, now?"

"I'm just asking some questions."

"Yeah, you are. You think you're gonna prove he's inno-cent before he can hang?"

"I guess we'll see."

Hastings sat forward.

"Look," he said, "try tellin' Miklin that this is all his son's fault. There's no point in blaming anybody else."

"Sure there is."

"Oh? And who would that be?"

Clint walked to the door and said, "Whoever really killed Roy Tillman."

As Clint left the office he heard Hastings getting out from behind his desk in a hurry. Moments later he came through the door, quickly. He looked around, as if he expected Clint to be down the street. But he was right there, bringing the lawman up short.

"Now wait a minute!" he said. "You can't just make a statement like that and walk out."

"Oh?"

"Are you sayin' you know who killed Tillman?"

"Don't you?" Clint asked.

"Dave Miklin did it," Hastings said. "What're you thinkin'?"

"I'm thinking Dave Miklin didn't do it."

"And what do you base that on?" Hastings asked. "His daddy's money?"

"My own judge of character."

"So you believe the kid when he says he didn't do it."

"Somebody has to believe him," Clint said. "Didn't it ever occur to you that you had the wrong man?"

"No," Hastings said, "It didn't."

"Well," Clint said, "let's see what I can find out."

As Clint stepped into the street and started across Sheriff Hastings called out, "Wait a minute. Is that what this whole scale thing is about? You're tryin' to hold up the hangin'?"

"I don't know," Clint said, "I just know there are certain parts that aren't doing their job."

Clint was almost all the way across the street when Hastings shouted, "Is that supposed to be me?"

Clint turned, smiled and said, "We were talking about a scale, weren't we, Sheriff?"

Chapter Twenty-One

Clint was surprised to see the woman standing in front of his hotel. She was tall, blonde, beautiful, and Henry Miklin's daughter, Belinda. She was wearing a blue dress that covered her from neck to ankles, but was doing nothing to hide the curves of her body.

"Miss Miklin," he said, when he got to the door. It was the end of a long day, and he didn't need to be dealing with this bitter woman's attitude.

"There you are," she said. "I've been waitin' for you forever."

"Have you? To what do I owe this pleasure?"

"Can we go somewhere and talk?"

"Saloon?" he suggested.

"Too public," she said. "How about your room?"

"That's okay with me, if you can stand the damage to your reputation."

"You don't have any idea what my reputation can stand," she said. "Shall we?"

Clint led the way through the lobby and up to the second floor, to his room. They passed Wainwright's door. The hangman would have to wait for him a little longer.

He unlocked the door and allowed her to enter first, then closed and locked it.

She turned and looked at him.

"Unless you want me to leave it open?"

"Oh, don't be stupid," she said.

"Then what's this about?" he asked.

"My brother," she said. "My father says you're gonna prove him innocent."

"I never promised that," he told her. "I said I'd look into it and he said, whichever way it went, he'd pay me."

"So you're doing it for the money?"

He wasn't. but said, "Why does anyone do anything?"

"Well, I'll pay you more." She reached into her drawstring purse—blue to match the dress—and came out with a wad of bills. She dropped them onto the bed.

"There's more where that came from," she said.

"And what are you paying me for?"

"To do the opposite."

"Prove him guilty?"

"Exactly."

"Your own brother?"

She made a rude noise with her mouth, to illustrate how she felt about that.

"He's more of a nuisance than anything else," she said. "He always has been. And I don't need him inheriting the ranch when my father dies."

"I see."

"Will you do it?"

"Well, unfortunately," Clint said, "I happen to think he *is* innocent."

"That doesn't matter," she said. "I just want you to prove he's guilty, however you have to do it. Or, even better yet, just let him hang."

Clint studied the woman, wondered how she had gotten to be as cold as she obviously was.

"Oh, don't look at me like that," she said. "I know what you're thinking. I'm a cold bitch."

"That's exactly what I was thinking."

"I grew up in a boy's club," she told him. "My father, my brother, even the damned foreman, I had to take a back seat to all of 'em. Well, I'm thru doin' that."

"I'm sorry you feel that way, but I'm not going to railroad him onto the gallows, or just sit back and let him hang because you're paying me."

"So what do you want?" she asked. "<u>More</u> money? More than money? How about this?"

She suddenly pulled the dress she was wearing open at the front. It was obviously not a spur of the moment act, but something she had planned to do, for she was completely naked beneath it.

"This is what men want, isn't it?" she asked. She cupped her large breasts in her hands, flicked the large, pink nipples with her thumbs. "Or this?" She moved her hands down to the golden patch between her legs. "How about if I rub it, get myself wet for you?"

Clint realized the woman was getting herself excited. It had nothing whatsoever to do with him, but with her own attitude, her own actions.

"Come on, Adams," she said, tossing the dress away so that she was completely naked. "Money and me, isn't that what men want? Cash and sex?"

And in that moment Clint got angry.

"You know," he said, unstrapping his gun, "you're right, you cold bitch, that's exactly what I want."

He walked to the bed, hung the gun belt on the post, and then undid his belt and the buttons of his trousers.

She watched while he kicked off his boots, got rid of his pants, and shirt, and underwear, until he was as naked as she was, his cock standing straight and hard.

Quickly, she closed the distance between and grabbed his hard penis.

"Come on, give it to me!" she said.

"I'm going to give it to you, all right!" he snapped back, and pushed her down on the bed.

Chapter Twenty-Two

Rusty was blonde, but Belinda was even moreso.

She was also bigger, and stronger.

As Clint grabbed her ankles to spread her she used her impressive leg muscles to try to resist him, but in the end he persisted and got his way. She was right about the fact that she was already wet. He spread her legs and drove his cock right into her, cleaving her cleanly and driving himself right to the hilt.

She gasped, her eyes widening, and then he started fucking her hard, with no regard for how the bed would stand up to it, or who heard the sound of her screaming—because that's what she did, she screamed as he drove in and out of her.

Then she started to shout at him.

"Is that all you've got?" she demanded. "My father fucks me harder than this!"

So he went at her with renewed vigor. He released her ankles, got on his knees on the bed, moved as close to her as he could, forcing her knees up to her chest. Fucking her that way, her legs were flailing in the air, although a time or two her heels would strike him on the upper back.

She reached up and laced her hands behind his neck, pulled his face to her and kissed him roughly, driving her tongue into his mouth.

But she was also still verbally sniping at him, although he couldn't understand everything she was saying. He finally decided to change position, so he withdrew and grabbed her, intending to flip her over. But this time she dug her heels into the mattress and fought him like a tiger. It became more of a wrestling match than anything else.

She gained the upper hands by underhanded means. She reached down and grasped his testicles in one hand, and his cock in the other. In that way she was able to get him onto his back, unless he wanted her to squeeze his balls, painfully.

Once she had *him* flipped over she swooped down and immediately swallowed his cock, still holding onto his balls with one hand. She took him deep into her mouth and then started sucking him wetly, massaging his testicles at the same time.

He reached down to cup her head in his hands, but did nothing to try and get away from her. Why would he? The sensations from her mouth and hands were glorious!

She moaned while sucking him, which sent vibrations through him. Soon the room was filled with the gulping, juicy sounds of her mouth gobbling him up.

Finally, when he thought she was going to finish him, he managed to pull away from her without losing his balls. Again they had a wrestling match, but this time he was able to flip her onto her belly, spread her legs and enter her wet pussy from behind.

He lifted her up onto her knees and then she quite willingly hiked her butt up and began to not only take his thrusts, but lean back into them so that, in time, the room was filled with the sound of their damp flesh smacking against each other. But Clint, because she was so smug and sure of herself, withdrew before he was done and, instead, ejaculated his seed onto her back. Then he quit the bed and left her there, down on her belly again, her back covered with sticky gobs.

"Well," she gasped, breathlessly, "I guess since you got what you wanted, you'll do it."

"Make sure your brother hangs?" he asked, while he pulled on his trousers.

"Yes, of course. What have we been talking about?"

"Not a chance."

"What?" She glared back at him over her shoulder. "Whatayou mean?"

"I mean," he said, donning his shirt, "that I'm going to do exactly what I told your father I would do, prove Dave innocent or guilty, whichever he is."

"And you think he's innocent."

"Yes I do."

"Why?"

"Because he told me so."

"Jesus, and you believe him?"

"I do, yeah."

He took his gun from the bedpost and strapped it on, then sat at the bottom of the bed to pull his boots back on.

"So then what was this about?" she asked, patting the bed.

"That," he said, "was me giving you what you needed, not taking what I wanted. There's a difference."

"You think I came here needing you to fuck me?" she demanded.

"I think you came here to buy me," he said, "but what you need was to be dominated."

"Ha!" she laughed "You think you just dominated me?"

"Well," he said, standing, "I'm not the one who needs help cleaning my back."

"You sonofa—hey, what are you doing?" she demanded, as he opened the door.

"I've got things to do," he said.

"Wha—you can't leave me like this!" she shouted. "Throw me a towel. Come back here and clean my back!"

"I'm sure you'll find a way to clean your own back," he said, and left. He knew all she had to do was roll over and clean herself with his sheets, but it was worth some soiled bed linens to leave her that way.

Chapter Twenty-Three

Clint was out of breath in the hall. He would much rather have remained in bed for some time, resting, but he thought he'd made his point.

On the other hand, he had planned to talk with Belinda Miklin, more calmly and at length, to see if she thought her brother was guilty. But apparently it didn't matter whether he *was* guilty or not, she *wanted* him to hang. So there wasn't much chance she would say anything that would do the young man any good.

So far he had spoken to the sister, the father, the sheriff who arrested him, the lawyer who defended him, and the prisoner, himself. And the only one he felt had said anything useful was Dave, the prisoner. And he tended to believe him. The question was, how to prove it?

He walked down the hall to Wainwright's door and knocked. He heard him remove the chair from beneath the doorknob, and then the door opened.

"I heard a woman screaming," he said, as Clint entered.

"Yeah, so did I," Clint said. "How are you doing?"

"I've been fiddlin' with the scale parts," he said. "Just in case the sheriff came by to check."

"He might be doing that," Clint said, "now that he knows I'm asking questions."

"He knows?"

"Well, he had to," Clint said. "I had to talk to him, and to the prisoner, himself."

"And who else?"

"Well, I spoke with his lawyer," Clint said. "He was no help. He thinks Dave did it."

"That's a shame."

"Yeah, it is. And then I spoke with Gina, the saloon girl, about the prisoner and victim supposedly fought over."

"Supposedly?"

"Her name is Evelyn. Apparently, she says she didn't know either of them. Not so they'd fight over her, that is. I still need to talk with her, but it sounds like I'd have to go through her father."

Wainwright looked dismayed.

"I don't think I should even be hearin' this," he said. "Guilt or innocence has never mattered to me before."

"But you're changing," Clint said. "You said so."

"That's true." Wainwright sat on the end of his bed. "Go on."

"Also talked with his sister, Belinda."

"Ah, we met her at the ranch."

"Yes."

"Beautiful woman," Wainwright said.

"Yes," Clint said, "but cold as ice. She wants her brother to hang, it doesn't matter to her whether he's innocent or guilty."

"But . . . why?"

"So she can inherit when her father dies," Clint said. "If Dave is alive then he inherits, and she'll probably be stuck living there and helping him. And according to everyone—the sister, the lawyer, even his father—the boy's an idiot. He'd never be able to run the business alone."

"So she'd be . . . like a prisoner."

"I suppose that's what she thinks," Clint said. "So she'd rather see him dead."

"So . . . do you think she framed him? Killed the other man herself? Or had him killed?'

"Those are all possibilities, I suppose," Clint said. "Or it could be that she just sees this going her way."

"So you're gonna see that it doesn't?"

"I have to admit," Clint said, "I'd like him to go free just to see the look on her face, but I admit I don't know how to do that, just yet."

"Well," Wainwright said, "we can't keep this scale thing going forever."

"No, I didn't think so," Clint said. "You'll just have to weight him tomorrow, which will give me the full day to work on this."

"And then the next day, I'll have to hang him," Wain-wright said.

"Yes, you will," Clint said. "If you're up to it. Do you think you are, Carl? Do you think you've got one more in you?"

"I honestly don't know," Wainwright said. "I guess we'll have to find out."

"Well," Clint said, "we've still got some time. If I prove him innocent, then you won't have to even make that decision."

"But I will have to make it, at some point."

"Yes," Clint said. "Think about it. And if the sheriff knocks on the door, let him in."

"Are you sure?" Wainwright asked.

"Yes," Clint said. "He's on the side that wants the boy hanged. Just answer his questions, if he comes. Tell him the scale will be ready tomorrow."

"A-all right. What are you going to do now?"

"It occurs to me I haven't been to the scene of the killing, yet," Clint said. "So I think I'll do that next."

"It's gettin' late," Wainwright told him. "I'm hungry."

"All right," Clint said, "change of plans. Let's go and get something to eat."

***

It was late, dark already, but they found a café that was open and ate tough steaks, underdone potatoes and carrots, washing it down with weak coffee. After, they went back to the hotel.

"The plan for tomorrow is the same," Clint told Wainwright, at his door. "We'll have breakfast, and then I'll go and take a look at where the murder took place. Hopefully, it will tell me something."

"The sheriff is sure to come lookin' for me in the meantime," the hangman said.

"Like I said, let him in," Clint said, "show him the parts, but assure him that you will have the prisoner weighed before the end of the day."

"He'll want to hang him the following day," Wainwright pointed out.

"Hopefully," Clint said, "I'll know what I need to know by then. Good-night, Carl."

"Good-night, Clint."

Chapter Twenty-Four

On the way out to supper Clint had informed the desk clerk his bed needed clean sheets. When he returned to his room he found the bed had been changed, and Belinda was gone. He undressed, reclined on the bed, too tired to read, he drifted off . . .

***

In the morning Clint could have gone back to the sheriff to find out where the murder had taken place, but he didn't want the lawman to know what he was doing, anymore. So after breakfast he sent the hangman back to his room and went to the lawyer, Cunningham, who not only agreed to tell him where it happened, but to take him there.

"Why not?" the man asked, getting up from behind his desk. "I've got nothing else to do."

"No new clients?"

"Not right now," he said. "In fact, I'm waiting to see if I still have a client."

"You mean Henry Miklin."

He nodded. "The old man might fire my ass if his boy hangs. So if showin' you where it happened keeps *that* from happening, I'm all for it."

They left the office and Cunningham led the way to an empty lot between two buildings in a rundown part of town.

"They're going to build this up, eventually, but right now it's just this space and some empty buildings."

"So why would two young men agree to meet here—when? At night?"

Cunningham nodded and said, "Late, probably. Nobody heard the shot. The body was just found the next morning by some kids who came here to play. Otherwise, who knows . . ." The lawyer shrugged. ". . . it might have laid here for days."

Clint studied the lot, walked it, looked around at the surrounding buildings.

"No chance of a witness, huh?" he asked.

"None."

"Well," Clint said, "the dead boy could have been lured here any number of ways—maybe a message to meet a girl?"

"Who knows?" Cunningham asked.

"Does he have family?"

"Just a mother," the lawyer said. "She's distraught and can't wait for Dave Miklin to swing."

"I guess I should go and see her. Maybe he told her why he was coming here."

"You're gonna be surprised."

"Why?"

"You'll see," Cunningham said. "She works at the Crosscreek Saloon."

"A saloon girl?"

"Like I said," Cunningham repeated, "you'll be surprised."

"You ready for a drink?" Clint asked.

"Always," the man said.

The Crosscreek Saloon was smaller than the Lodge Saloon and looked a little older. The buildings surrounding it had some age to them.

"It's open this early?" Clint asked.

"It's always open," Cunningham said.

"This looks like an older part of town," Clint said.

"This is the original section of town," Cunningham told him.

"And you? Are you from here?"

"I came here a few years ago from St. Louis. I met Miklin there doing some business, and he convinced me to come here and work for him. Now I may be out of a job."

They entered the saloon, the hinges of the batwing doors squeaking to announce their arrival. But there were only a few patrons in the place, and only two or three of them turned to look.

Clint glanced around, didn't see any saloon girls working the empty floor. Then he looked at the bar again and saw the woman working behind it.

"The bartender?" he asked.

"That's right," Cunningham said. "A lady bartender. That's Dani Tillman."

The woman was wearing a long sleeved shirt, with the sleeves rolled up to show strong forearms. She was a meaty woman in her late 40s or early 50s, but she had a mass of flaming red hair, sparkling green eyes, full breasts, and he could see what a beauty she had been when she was younger.

J.R. Roberts

Cunningham led the way to the bar, where the lady bartender was leaning on her elbows, looking bored—or sad. When she saw the lawyer, her face lit up just a bit—in recognition more than pleasure. After all, he had been the lawyer trying to get Dave Miklin acquitted of killing her son.

"Mr. Cunningham," she said. "What can I do for you?"

"Dani—"

"Mrs. Tillman to you, Counselor."

"All right," he said. "Mrs. Tillman, this is Clint Adams."

She gave Clint a hard look.

"I heard you was in town," she said. "You're gonna make sure the hangman lives to hang my boy."

"That's not exactly true," Clint said, "but since you brought it up, I don't suppose you had anything to do with bushwhacking him outside of town?"

"Oh yeah, I did."

"What?" Cunningham said.

"Just look around," she said, waving her hands and ignoring Cunningham. "I got all these folks who are willin' to help me."

They looked around, but nobody was paying them any attention.

"Would you be willing to answer a few questions?" Clint asked.

"So you can try to get my boy's killer off?" she asked.

"I just want to make sure the right person gets hanged, Ma'am," Clint said.

She glared at him for a moment, then shrugged and said, "Go ahead and ask. I can't guarantee I'll answer all of 'em."

94

"Fair enough," Clint said.

Chapter Twenty-Five

"Did your son say who he was meeting that night?" Clint asked.

"Not a damned word. Next question?"

"Did you know anything about the fight he had over the girl, Evelyn Hargrove?"

"No. Roy didn't talk to me a lot."

"Did you know who his friends were?"

"He was nineteen," she said. "I assume his friends were other nineteen-year olds. Look, my boy was no angel, and he didn't talk much, but he was my boy. I want whoever killed him to hang. I don't care if it's Dave Miklin or somebody else. But the court said it was Miklin. What makes you think different? His pa's money?"

"I talked to the boy. He says he didn't do it and I believe him. It's got nothing to do with money. I don't want an innocent boy to hang, do you?"

"No," she said, quickly, "I don't."

"Mrs. Tillman—"

"Just call me Dani," she told him. To the lawyer she added, "I'm still Mrs. Tillman to you."

"Yes, Ma'am," Cunningham said.

"Dani," Clint said, "Gina, the saloon girl, told me Evelyn really didn't know either boy very well—certainly not well enough for them to fight over her. Why would Roy go into the Lodge Saloon and start a fight over a girl he hardly knew?"

"Maybe he was drunk."

"Did he drink here?"

"Not if I was workin' the bar. Another bartender, maybe, but I was workin' that night."

"From what I heard he didn't have that many drinks in the Lodge before the fight."

"There's lots of places to get a drink," she said.

"So what if somebody got him drunk, and sent him in there to start that fight? Could he be influenced like that?"

"If you're askin' me if he was dumb enough for that to happen, well, yeah. He was nineteen!"

"Do you truly think Dave killed Roy, or are you just going along with the court's decision?"

"What else am I supposed to do?" she asked, with a shrug. "Ain't we supposed believe the courts?"

"Most of the time," Clint said, "but sometimes, they get it wrong."

Dani suddenly looked uncomfortable behind the bar.

"What do you want me to say?"

"I just want you to consider that somebody else possibly killed your son. And who you think that might be. Can you do that?"

After a moment she said, "I'll do it. I wanna get it right for my boy."

"Thank you," Clint said. "I don't have much time to do this, so I'd like to come back and talk to you, soon."

"Come back any time, Gunsmith," she said. "I'll be here."

Clint nodded, and he and Cunningham left the saloon.

***

Outside Clint said, "The sheriff must have talked to the hangman by now."

"So when will it be?"

"Probably tomorrow."

"So you have to prove it today," the lawyer said. "Either he did it, or he didn't."

"Do you know any of Roy Tillman's friends?"

"No."

"Do you know any of Dave Miklin's friends?"

"That's different," Cunningham said. "I know a few of them. But why talk to his friends?"

"Because," Clint said, "it may turn out that one or more of his friends are also his enemies."

Chapter Twenty-Six

Cunningham gave Clint 3 names, but told him he'd probably find all 3 in the same place.

"And where's that?" he asked, as they walked back to the center of town.

"Since they're too young for a saloon," the lawyer said, "you'll find them together in an abandoned building with a bottle of whiskey."

"An abandoned building where?"

"Not far from where the body was found."

"Wait a minute," Clint said, "Dave Miklin drank with them, there?"

Cunningham shrugged. "He must've. They were his friends."

"And did Roy Tillman drink with them?"

"Dave told me no."

"And you believed him."

"He was my client," Cunningham said. "I had to believe him."

'Jesus Christ," Clint said.

"What?"

"If they were all friends together, drinking together, then Tillman's death was the result of something that happened between them."

"Why do you say that?"

"Because they're nineteen years old!" Clint said.

"Dave insists Tillman wasn't part of their group."

"Because if he said he was, that would give him more of a motive."

"So you're thinking one of the others might have had a motive to kill Tillman, and pin it on Dave."

"That's what I'm going to find out," Clint told him.

"I'll go with you," Cunningham said.

"No, go back to your office," Clint said. "I might need to frighten them, and I can do that better alone."

"Suit yourself," Cunningham said. "Just let me know what you find out, because I'll probably have to be the one to present it to the law."

"Don't worry," Clint said. "You'll be the first to know."

***

Clint walked back to the empty lot where Tillman's body had been found, then started checking the abandoned buildings around it. He didn't find anyone drinking, but he did find one that had a lot of empty bottles in it. It looked like it used to be a hardware store, for there were nails and screws scattered about on the floor.

It was probably too early in the day for them to be there, drinking. They were probably out looking for bottles. And who could be more helpful to them than a bartender?

He decided to go back and see Dani Tillman a little earlier than planned.

The Crosscreek Saloon was busier than it had been before, but not by much. Dani was still leaning on the bar, looking bored. She perked up a bit when Clint reentered, straightened up and watched him as he approached the bar.

"Back so soon?" she asked.

"I'm sorry but I thought of more questions."

"Well, thanks for leavin' that lawyer behind," she said. "I don't have much use for him."

"He was only doing his job when he defended young Miklin."

"I suppose so. You want a beer?"

He shook his head. 'Too early."

"How about a coffee?"

"That'd be good."

"I have a pot in my office," she said.

"So you own this place?"

"Oh yeah," she said, "Owner, bartender, and swamper. I do it all. It's always been that way. My boy wasn't much help. Come on, follow me."

She came out from behind the bar and led him across the room, pausing only to say, "Stan watch the bar—and no free drinks!"

Her office was a small room at the back. They went through the door and she closed it firmly behind her.

"This is my sanctuary," she said. "The only place I can get any peace. Nobody wants anythin' from me back here."

He noticed, in the small room, that she smelled very good. And the room's scent was a mixture of her, and the coffee. Heady for a man who liked both.

She moved gracefully to the coffee pot. She was tall, full-breasted, had spread out a bit in the waist and butt, but not unpleasantly so.

She poured two cups of coffee and handed him one, then stood there in front of him rather than go behind her desk.

"So what other questions have you come up with?" she asked him.

"First, have you done what I asked?"

"I've been thinkin', sure, but I can't come up with anybody who'd want to kill my boy. Why would anybody want to kill somebody as useless as he was?"

"I understand that there was a group of boys his age who used to meet in an abandoned building to drink together."

"Really?"

"They were friends of Dave Miklin's," Clint said. "Do you know if your son was part of this group?"

"Well, he had friends," she said, "and I know he drank, so who knows?"

"You said you never gave him whiskey."

"That's right," she said, "or beer, before you ask." She sipped her coffee, regarded him above the rim with those startling green eyes.

"What about Dave Miklin? Or the other boys? They must have been getting their whiskey from somewhere."

"No," she said, "I'm not in the habit of giving teenage boys whiskey. If they were gettin' it from a bartender, it's another one."

"Okay."

"Anything else?"

"No," Clint said, "I'm just flailing around right now, looking for something to hang onto."

"I've got somethin' you can hang onto," she said.

"What's that?"

"Me," she said. "I thought you might be interested in fucking me on my desk before you leave."

Chapter Twenty-Seven

It wasn't as if the thought hadn't crossed his mind. She was an older woman who still projected sex with those eyes, that hair and body. But it really hadn't been on his mind when he followed her back to her office.

But it was on his mind now.

He moved closer to her in the small office and she came into his arms. They shared a kiss that went on for a long time and seemed to seal the deal that this was going to happen.

She stepped back from him, then, and unbuttoned her shirt. As he watched her peel off her clothes he removed his own shirt, dropped his trousers to his ankles. He didn't see any reason to remove his boots because what was going to happen here was going to happen hard and fast, and there was no bed involved. He did, however, remove his gun belt and set it aside within easy reach. He recalled her locking the office door, but somebody could certainly kick it in.

He took in her nudity, full breasts with brown nipples, freckled cleavage. Her skin was smooth, her waist and butt had filled as she got older, and there was a slight fold of skin around her middle, but as a total package the woman oozed sex.

Especially her scent.

As she sat up on the desk and spread her legs he could see the wetness in the red forest between her thighs. He was full and hard as he stepped to her, pressed the head of his cock to her wet pussy lips, and slid right in.

She gasped as he pierced her, sliding in to the hilt so that their pubic bushes intertwined.

"Yes," she said, leaning back to take her weight on her hands set behind her. Those large breasts, not as high and firm as they had probably been some years back, splayed to either side a bit, but that didn't dissuade him from leaning over, kissing her nipples and taking them into his mouth. After that he simply stood up straight as she spread her knees and he began to fuck her hard and fast, which was obviously just what she wanted.

"Oh yes," she said, again, "do it, make it hard and good, come on . . ."

The desk began to move, and he wondered for a moment if anyone out in the saloon could hear what was going on. But the room was small, so soon enough the desk hit the wall and, from that point on, stopped moving, except for an occasional jump.

As he continued to drive into her she took her weight off her hands and leaned forward, wrapped her arms around his neck and held on for dear life.

He held onto the edge of the desk and continued to slam into her, as she pulled with her arms to come forward and meet each thrust. At the point where he started to feel a strain on his neck she suddenly released him, and leaned back as the pleasure washed over her, and then he exploded. She did everything she could—biting her lips, whipping her head to one side and, at one point, actually biting her own shoulder—to keep from screaming . . .

***

"My God!" she said as they got dressed. "We're gonna have to try that on a bed before you leave town."

"Sounds like a good idea to me," he agreed, strapping on his gun.

She did what she could to fix her hair, but no matter what she did it was a mass of red waves.

"You probably think I'm a hell of a lousy mother, rutting in my office while my boy lies in the ground."

"Not at all," Clint said. "It didn't sound like you and Roy had a close connection."

"He took after his lazy bum of a father."

"Where is his father?"

"He got himself killed by falling asleep on the main road one night. The stage came by and drove right over him. The only thing he left me was this place. He'd driven it almost into the ground. I've managed to keep it going."

"I admire that," he said.

"Thanks. Oh, I forgot, we came back here for coffee."

It had gotten cold in the cups.

"That's okay," he said, "what I got made up for it."

"Not bad for an old broad, huh?"

"Not bad for any age, Dani. You're quite a woman."

"I hope things go the way you want them, Clint," she said.

"What I want, Dani," he said, "is the person who actually killed your son to pay for it. If it turns out that it was Dave Miklin, well, so be it."

Chapter Twenty-Eight

Clint returned to the empty lot later in the day, then went back to the building where he had found some remnants of drinking. Sure enough, standing outside the door he heard what could only be described as drunken bluster from inside.

He entered as quietly as he could and saw 3 boys about Dave Miklin's age sitting in a circle and passing a bottle of whiskey around. He wanted to make an immediate impression on them, and get them talking. So he did something he hardly ever did. He drew his gun and fired one shot. The bottle in the hand of one of the boys shattered, and all 3 boys froze. He had fired for effect, and had achieved it. He holstered the gun, reminding himself to eject the spent shell later and replace it.

"Now that I have your attention," he said, "don't anybody move."

"J-jesus, Mister!" said the boy who had been holding the bottle. "You coulda s-shot my h-hand off!"

"No chance of that, son," Clint said. "If I had wanted to shoot off your hand, I would've."

"Who the hell are you?" one of the other boys asked.

"My name is Clint Adams."

He waited to see if they'd recognize him. After all, they were pretty young, but one of them raised his eyebrows and pointed.

"T-that's the Gunsmith!" he blurted.

"It ain't not," another said. "There ain't no such person."

"Did you see the way he shot that bottle outta my hand?" the first boy said. "He's the Gunsmith. I heard he was in town for the hangin'."

"That right?" the doubtful boy asked. "You're here for the hangin'?"

"Sort of."

"What's that mean?" the boy who had been holding the bottle asked.

"It means I want to make sure the right boy is being hanged."

"You don't think Dave did it?" the first boy asked.

"Before we get into this," Clint said. "What are your names? First names, only."

In turn they said, "Jay," "Bart," "Sam." Those were the three names Cunningham had given him.

The boy who had been holding the bottle was Sam.

"Okay," Clint said, "let's settle down and talk about this."

"Why?" Bart asked. He was the doubtful boy. Clint thought he might have to prove himself to this one, again. "Why should we talk to you? Why shouldn't we just leave?" Clint figured he was the drunker of the three, because he had the biggest mouth.

"If you try to walk out of here before I let you I'll shoot your finger off."

Bart frowned. "Which one?"

"You pick."

Bart stared at him.

"I'd like to see that," Jay said. "Go ahead, Bart, try to leave."

"Shut up!" Bart said.

"Can we talk?" Clint asked.

"Yeah," Bart said, "so talk."

"Dave used to drink here with you right?"

"Right," Sam said.

Bart glared at him.

"What? We said we're gonna talk." He pointed. "He's the Gunsmith, for Chrissake!"

"What about Roy?" Clint asked.

All three boys looked at him

"Did Roy drink with you fellas?"

"Sometimes," Jay said.

"Why only sometimes?"

"Him and Dave didn't like each other," Bart said.

"Do you three think Dave actually killed Roy?" Clint asked.

"The judge and jury said he did," Bart said. "That's good enough for me."

"What about you two?" Clint asked Jay and Sam. "Does Bart speak for you two?"

"No, he don't speak for me," Jay said. "Look, Dave was— is my friend. I don't want him to hang for . . . for killing Roy."

"Why not?" Clint asked. "Because he didn't do it?"

"We don't know if he did it or not," Sam said. "Not for sure anyway."

"But you don't think he did it."

"Why would he?" Sam asked. "He didn't even know that girl."

"Did Roy know her?"

Bart laughed. "Roy was afraid to talk to girls."

"And he wasn't your friend," Clint said.

"No," Bart said. "He wanted to be in our group, but we didn't want him."

"You didn't want him," Sam said, "and neither did Dave."

"So Bart and Dave didn't like him?"

"No," Jay said, "they didn't."

"So that gives Dave a motive to kill him," Clint said.

"I-I guess," Jay said.

Clint pointed. "And it gives Bart, here, the same motive. Doesn't it?"

Sam and Jay looked at Bart.

Chapter Twenty-Nine

"You're crazy!" Bart blurted. "I'm gettin' outta here!"

Bart started across the room, but Clint got in his way and put his hand out.

"Don't make me draw my gun again," he said.

Bart stopped.

"I didn't kill Roy!"

"But do you know who did?" Clint asked.

Bart looked at Jay and Sam.

"Don't look at us," Jay said.

"Yeah, we didn't do it," Sam said. "You're the one who didn't like 'im."

"That don't mean I killed him!" Bart yelled. He looked at Clint. "What's Dave sayin'? Is he sayin' I did it?"

"What if he is?"

"Then he's lyin'"

"He didn't mention you in court, did he?" Clint asked.

"N-no . . ."

"So what makes you think he'd be mentioning you now?" Clint asked.

"'cause he don't wanna hang!" Bart said. "He'd probably try to pin it on anybody."

"Well, he hasn't," Clint said. "He hasn't mentioned any of your names. All he's saying is that he didn't do it."

The three boys looked at each other.

"I guess he thinks of you as good friends," Clint said.

"Yeah, well," Bart said, "we are."

"Then I'd think you'd want to help him."

"We do," Jay said.

"So then tell me," Clint said, "who else would want to kill Roy Tillman?"

They looked at each other again, and then Jay said, "We don't know."

"Okay, then tell me this," Clint said, "who should I look at other than you three."

"Why us three?" Jay asked.

"Because you haven't given me anybody else."

"What about his mother?" Bart asked.

"Dani Tillman?"

"Yeah," Bart said, "they didn't get along."

"But why would she kill him?"

"Because he was just like his dad," Bart said, "and she hated his dad."

"Some people think she killed his dad," Jay said

"I thought he was run over by a stage coach."

"Yeah," Sam said, "that's how it looked. But some people think he was already dead when he got run over."

"Okay, there, you see?" Clint said. "Now we're getting somewhere."

"We got another bottle," Sam said. "You wanna drink with us?"

"Sure," Clint said, "open it up." He smiled. "Let's pass it around."

Halfway through the bottle Jay said, "You ain't so bad, ya know?"

"Thanks," Clint said.

The boys were drinking eagerly from the bottle, while Clint took small sips. He wanted to get them drunker to see what else they would say.

So far they had mentioned Roy's mother, Roy's Uncle Al, and a man named George Hargrove, who had a 16 year old daughter. The Uncle was Roy's father's brother, who Dani Tillman also hated. Hargrove's daughter was pretty, and Roy had a crush on her.

"But you said Roy was afraid to talk to girls," Clint reminded them.

"Oh, he was," Jay said, "but he used to follow her around all the time."

"It made her nervous," Sam said.

"More like scared," Jay added.

"So you think her father might've killed him?" Clint asked them.

They shrugged, almost in unison.

"You just said you wanted some other names," Bart said, "so we're givin' 'em to ya."

They were all drunk, but Bart was seriously slurring his words. Clint guessed he didn't have much longer to be making sense, or even to be awake. In fact, he was nodding off, even now.

"So," he said, "any other names?"

"No," Sam said.

Jay shook his head

113

Bart snored.

Clint stood up, still holding half a bottle of whiskey in his left hand.

"Okay," he said, "thanks for talking to me."

"Whataya gonna do?" Jay asked.

"I'm going to find out who killed Roy," Clint said. "And if I find out it was one of you, God help you."

"It wasn't!" Sam said.

"If you leave town I'll assume it was, and I'll come after you, so just stay put. Do you all live in town?"

"No," Jay said, "I do, with my uncle. He runs the general store."

"I live outside of town, with my mother," Sam said. "She's a drunk."

Clint looked at Bart, who was now deeply asleep, his chin on his chest.

"What about Bart?"

"He lives by himself," Sam said.

"How old is he?"

"We're all nineteen," Jay said, "but Bart, he's twenty-one."

"So he gets the whiskey?"

"Yah," Jay said.

"Okay, then," Clint said. "I'll talk to you all again."

He started for the door.

"Hey!" Sam shouted.

"What?" Clint turned.

"The bottle," Jay said.

"Oh." Clint tossed it to them, making sure it landed between them and smashed on the floor. "Oops."

Chapter Thirty

Clint went to see Sheriff Hastings. The lawman wasn't in the office, so he started checking saloons. He found him in the Lodge.

"On my rounds," Hastings said, "stopped in for a beer. Want one?"

"Sure."

Hastings waved, and the bartender brought Clint a beer.

"You lookin' for me?" the lawman asked.

"I was." He sipped the beer.

"What for?"

"I've been talking to people around town, coming up with some names of people who might've killed Roy Tillman."

"Is that right?"

"Yeah. I thought I'd run some of them by you."

The place was doing a brisk business and was noisy.

"Let's go to the end of the bar," Hastings said.

They walked to the end near the front window. Clint made sure he was standing with Sheriff Hastings between him and the front.

"I heard something about a man named George Hargrove," Clint said.

"George? What about him?"

"I heard his daughter was afraid of Roy."

"Evelyn? She's not afraid of him. She feels—felt sorry for him."

"And her father?"

"George didn't like the boy, but he didn't kill him."

"How do you know that?"

"Because I know George," he said. "He's a businessman here in town. He wouldn't risk all that just to kill a boy who was lovesick over Evelyn. If he was gonna do that, he'd have to kill half the boys in town."

"Is she pretty?"

"Like an angel."

"So I guess you don't think she killed him?"

Hastings laughed. "No, of course not."

"Then you wouldn't mind if I talk to them?"

"I don't care," Hastings said. "If you think you have the time."

"Speaking of that," Clint said, "I'll check with Wainwright about that scale. I'll bet we can come over later tonight and weigh him."

"That'll be fine," Hastings said. "We can get this hangin' done tomorrow."

"Think you can let everyone in town know by then?"

"Believe me, the whole town's waitin'," he said. "It won't take long. Are those the only names you have?"

"No," Clint said, "I heard something about Roy's uncle. His father's brother?"

"Naw, naw," Hastings said, "if it had been his mother, Dani, who was killed, then I'd suspect Al Stillwell. He thinks Dani killed his brother. But Dave's Uncle Al wasn't even in town at the time."

"Would he kill her son to get even?" Clint asked.

Hastings scratched his jaw.

"I always thought Al liked Roy, but . . . who knows?"

"So you never asked him?"

"Well, no," the lawman said. "His name never came up during the court case."

"And then there's Dani herself."

"Killin' her own son? They weren't close, but I can't see a mother killin' her own son . . . can you?"

"Probably not, since I've now met her," Clint said.

"She's quite a woman," Hastings said.

"Yes, she is," Clint agreed.

"Is that it?"

"Yes," Clint said. "I'll have to talk to Hargrove and Al Tillman tonight."

"Go right ahead. And see about that scale, will ya? The mayor's askin' me when this is gonna get done."

"Sure," Clint said. "I'll go over to the hotel now and check."

"I'll be at the office as soon as I finish this beer."

Clint drank some more of his own beer, then put the half empty mug on the bar, and left the saloon.

Chapter Thirty-One

"Well, sure," Wainwright said. "We only have to go to the livery, put these parts back on the scale and then drive it over to the jail."

"We'll have to take him out of his cell and to your wagon, right?"

"Yes."

"All right, I guess we better do that before it gets much later," Clint said. "Then I have some more people to talk to."

"You're gonna pursue this right down to the last minute, aren't you?"

"Yes," Clint said. "I'm becoming more and more sure the kid didn't do it."

"Well then, I guess you better prove it pretty quick."

***

They left the hotel, went to the stable, where Wainwright reassembled the scale.

"We could carry it into the sheriff's office, but it's pretty heavy. Better if we bring the prisoner to it."

So they hooked the horse up to the wagon and drove it over to the sheriff's office.

"About time," Hastings said, when they entered. "Where is it?"

"Outside," Wainwright said. "We'll have to bring the prisoner to the wagon."

"What? You can't bring it in here?"

"It's pretty heavy," Clint said.

"Well, okay," Hastings said, "but I'll have to bring him out."

"Fine," Wainwright said.

The lawman went into the cell block. Unlocked the cell and brought Dave Miklin out.

"What's goin' on?" the boy demanded. "Where are we goin'?" He looked at Clint and Wainwright.

"Just outside, to my wagon," the hangman said. "It's time to weigh you."

Miklin sighed. "Okay, let's get this over with."

They all walked outside. Clint noticed that Hastings had manacled Miklin's hands in front of him.

At the wagon Wainwright said, "I'll have to take him into the wagon and weigh him. You and Clint can wait out here."

"I want to watch," Hastings said.

"That's fine," Wainwright said. "I'll keep the door open. Oh, I'll need his manacles removed."

"Why?"

"They will affect his weight."

"Oh, all right," Hastings said. He undid the manacles and said to Miklin, "If you try to run I'll shoot you in the knee, and you'll still hang tomorrow."

The boy just nodded and stepped up into the wagon.

Manipulating the weights and counterweights on the scale Wainwright weighed the prisoner, then looked out at Clint and smiled.

"One seventy-six," he said.

"When they arrested me I weighed one ninety-one," Miklin complained. "They're starvin' me."

"You won't have to worry about that for much longer," Hastings told him. "Let's go, back to your cell."

"Hold on a second," Clint said. "Dave, I talked to Bart, Jay and Sam."

"So?"

"Bart didn't like Roy," Clint said. "Do you think he could've killed him?"

"Bart's all talk."

"What about Roy's mother?" Clint asked. "Could she have killed him?"

"Roy and his mother weren't close, but I can't see her killin' him. She's a decent woman."

"What about Roy's Uncle Al?"

"What about him?"

"He hates Roy's mother," Clint said. "Would he have killed Roy and framed you to get back at her?"

"I doubt it. Al and Roy were close."

"All right, let's go. Back to your cell," Hastings said.

"One more!" Clint said, holding out his hand. "George Hargrove, Dave."

"Evelyn's daddy?" he asked. "Yeah, that makes sense. He hated Roy 'cause he followed her everywhere."

"Okay, I'm going to talk to him."

"Do you really think you can find the real killer?" Miklin asked.

"I just know I'm going to be trying, Dave," Clint replied.

Right to the end, huh?" Sheriff Hastings asked. "Come on, Miklin."

Wainwright stepped out of the wagon while Hastings took Miklin back into the jail.

"Now what?" he asked.

"Let's get this wagon back to the livery, and you back to your room," Clint said. "I've got more people to talk to."

Chapter Thirty-Two

George Hargrove lived in a house on the outskirts of town, with his daughter Evelyn. As he approached it, Clint realized he hadn't asked whether or not there was a Mrs. Hargrove, or if the father and daughter lived alone? He would have to find that out after he knocked.

Wainwright was back in the hotel, barricaded in his room, even though he had asked to come along. Clint didn't want to take the chance somebody would take a shot at him. He had come to the conclusion that the sheriff wasn't looking for the bushwhacker at all, so they were still out there.

He stepped up onto the small house's worn porch and knocked on the door. A large, florid faced man in his 50s opened it and glared at Clint.

"Whataya want?"

"My name is—"

"I know who you are," the man said, cutting him off. "Everybody in town knows who you are and what you're doin' here. Whataya want from me?"

"Can I come in?"

"You're the damn Gunsmith," he said. "Can I stop you?"

"Sure, you can," Clint said. "This is your house. If you say no, it's no."

The man stared at him, then stepped back and said, "Come on in, then."

Clint entered the small but neatly kept house.

"I hope I'm not disturbing your wife," Clint said.

"No wife," the man said, "just me and my daughter."

"Evelyn, isn't it?"

Hargrove frowned. "That's right. Why do you know my daughter's name?"

"I understand she was being . . . bothered by Roy Tillman before he was killed."

"That boy was troubled," Hargrove said. "Unhappy. Had no friends. He started following her."

"Did you speak with him?"

"I did," Hargrove said. "I told him I'd break his neck if he didn't leave my daughter alone."

"But he didn't die from a broken neck, did he?"

"No," Hargrove said, "he got himself shot. And not by me, if that's what you're thinkin'."

"Not even to protect your daughter?"

"That boy wasn't a danger to her," Hargrove said, "he was a bother."

"So she wasn't afraid of him?"

"Not at all."

"Would you mind if I heard that from her?"

Hargrove's face grew red.

"You think I'm lyin'?"

"Not at all," Clint said. "There just might be something she can tell me that nobody else has."

"What are you tryin' to do?"

"I'm trying to make sure the right person hangs, Mr. Hargrove. You wouldn't want an innocent boy to go to the gallows, would you?"

"Well, no, but the judge and jury—" "Have been wrong before," Clint finished. "Please, just a few minutes."

"If she says it's okay," the man said.

"That's fair enough."

"I'll ask her."

He went into one of the back rooms, and Clint heard two voices murmuring. Finally, Hargrove came out with a pretty blonde girl behind him. Sheriff Hastings had been right. The girl looked like an angel.

"Evie," Hargrove said, "this is Mr. Adams."

"Yes, I know," she said, her blue eyes very bright. "The Gunsmith. It's very exciting to meet you, Mr. Adams."

"I'm happy to meet you, too, Evelyn."

"Just call me Evie," she insisted.

"All right, Evie," Clint said. "Did your dad tell you why I'm here?"

She nodded. "You're trying to keep Dave Miklin from hanging."

"I'm trying to do that if it turns out he's innocent," Clint clarified.

"How do you think I can help?"

"The word is going around town that, even though the boys were supposed to have been fighting over you, you actually didn't know either of them."

"Well, I knew them on sight, from school and around town," she admitted, "but I didn't know either one well."

"Even though Roy Tillman used to follow you?"

"But he never talked to me," she said, "and I never said nothing to him."

"Was there any way you can see that Roy might have thought you were his girlfriend?"

"Maybe if he was crazy, or something."

"And the same with Dave Miklin?"

"I don't think he's crazy," she said, "but he's rich. Why would he wanna bother with me?"

"Well, you're very pretty."

"Thank you, but there are a lot of pretty girls in town."

"So you can't come up with one reason why these two boys would fight over you?"

"Mr. Adams," she said, "I truly don't understand boys, at all."

"Well," Clint said, "I'm sure many of the boys feel the same way about you, Evie." If she was lying about any part of what she'd said, he couldn't tell. She was either being truthful, or she was a great liar.

"Thank you for talking to me, Evie," Clint said. "I appreciate it. Mr. Hargrove?" He put his hand out and Evie's father shook it. "Thanks."

Hargrove walked him to the door, opened it and said, "I hope, if the boy is innocent, you can prove it."

"I hope so, too," Clint said. "I'd hate to think of an innocent young man being hanged while the whole town watches—most of them enjoying the show."

"People are mad," Hargrove said. "My Evie and me, we won't be there."

"Mr. Hargrove—"

"Just call me George."

"If there's anything you'd like to tell me," Clint said, "now is the time."

"Wait. You still think—" The man's face grew red again. "Why don't you just go back to calling me Mr. Hargrove." He slammed the door.

"Yessir," Clint said, and walked away.

Chapter Thirty-Three

Clint hated to think that a 16 year old girl might be lying to him, and doing it very well. He was confident in his ability to tell when someone wasn't being honest with him. He felt that George Hargrove had something he wasn't telling him, but Evie looked and sounded like she was telling the truth. If she wasn't, he was going to be very disappointed.

When he got back to the hotel he knocked on Wainwright's door.

"Let's get some supper," he said, when Wainwright opened the door.

***

They went to the same small café as the night before.

"What are you gonna do now?" the hangman asked, after they had ordered.

"I don't know."

"That boy's gonna hang tomorrow," Wainwright said, "and there ain't much I can do about it."

"I suppose the gallows could malfunction," Clint said.

"I inspected them," Wainwright reminded him. "I said they were okay."

"They could still malfunction," Clint said. "Or the rope could snap."

"The rope!" Wainwright said. "I gotta inspect the rope, inch-by-inch, to be sure that don't happen."

"So what if it does?"

"Then I buy a new one and try again," Wainwright said. "Meanwhile, my reputation would suffer. Same if the gallows don't work."

"Damage to your profession as an executioner, you mean?"

"Well, yeah."

"A profession you're not even sure you want to continue with?"

"Well . . . yeah."

"This might make stopping easier," Clint said.

"Maybe." Wainwright didn't look happy. "Do you really think the boy is innocent?"

"I do."

"And it's not his father's money?"

"I'm not even going to take his money," Clint said.

"Then what are you gonna do? Do you have any idea at all who might have killed the other boy?"

"I have an idea that I don't like," Clint said.

"What's that?"

"I think I've talked to everybody I can talk to," Clint said, "and only one person fits the bill. He may not be the actual killer, but he's got some interest in seeing Dave hang."

"Who's that?"

"Sheriff Hastings."

"The sheriff?" Wainwright asked. "What would he have to gain?"

"I don't know," Clint said, "but he's not doing a thing to find the men who ambushed you. And he seems in an all fired hurry for Miklin to hang. Like you he's supposed to be uninvolved, emotionally."

"He doesn't seem that emotional to me."

"Well, seems to me he wants this hanging to go off more than just as a lawman. That's my feeling, anyway."

"Any other feelings?" the hangman asked.

"Well, yes," Clint said. "I think George Hargrove knows something he's not telling me."

"Like what?"

"I don't know."

"So what are you gonna do?"

"Ask him again," Clint said. "Look, what time was the original hanging supposed to happen?"

"Nine a.m.," Wainwright said.

"Can you put it off 'til afternoon?" Clint asked. "Maybe something about the rope, or the gallows?"

"I'll do what I can," Wainwright said.

***

After supper they walked back to the hotel in the dark. There was a lamp every so often on the street, but for the most part it was dark. At that time of night there were no other people around.

"Wait," Clint said, putting his hand out to stop Wainwright.

"What is it?"

"Quiet."

Clint listened intently, and when he heard a familiar sound he yelled to Wainwright, "Get down!"

He tackled the hangman around the waist, and the momentum took them through the locked door of a leather shop just as the firing started.

Bullets broke the windows on either side of the door, showering them with glass as they lay on the floor inside.

Clint got to his knees and returned fire, in the hopes of causing a lull in the barrage. It worked. The firing stopped. He grabbed Wainwright and pulled him toward the back of the store.

"Go out the back!" he said. "I'll keep them busy."

"What about you?"

"They're after you, Carl!"

"But what if there's no back door?"

"Use a window! Get back to your hotel room and wait there."

He pushed Wainwright into a back room just as the firing started, again.

Clint went flat on the floor again, rolled into his back, and fed live rounds into his gun. He wondered if anyone would come running when and if they heard the shots—like the sheriff?

This had to be the bushwhackers, which meant it might be his only chance to catch them. He figured if he fired again it might invite another return barrage, during which he could duck out the back and, possibly, work his way around behind them. Since Wainwright was gone and safe, it was worth a try.

He rose up high enough to be seen and fired several shots. He wanted to make sure he was visible behind the muzzle flash. When they saw him they started firing again, and he took off. He could hear the breaking of more glass and chewing up the inside of the store, and he felt bad for the owner when he came to work the next morning.

As it turned out, there was a back door, and the hangman had left it open. Clint went out and made his way to the alley alongside the building. He could still hear shots as he worked his way to the street. Once there he saw there was no way to get behind them. But it was dark enough for him to possibly creep from the alley without being seen. Then he might be able to work his way down the street, and across.

He waited for the second barrage of shots to cease, which probably meant they were reloading. He slipped from the alley and, keeping close to the buildings, moved along down the street. When he felt he'd moved far enough away, he hurriedly ran across. Again, keeping close to the storefronts, he moved up the street until he was almost across from the leather store's battered front.

He heard a murmur of voices, and the sound of weapons being reloaded. He realized that the shooters were inside a couple of the storefronts. It was too dark for him to see what the businesses were, and he didn't know how many shooters there were, but if it was bushwhackers, there were 5.

"Where are they?" he heard someone say.

"Quiet! Just keep your eye on the door."

Those two voices came from the storefront closest to him. There was an alley alongside. He ducked in, hoping to get to the rear and inside before they decided to leave.

He found a back door which had been jimmied open, obviously by the shooters. As he found himself in a back storeroom. He waited some seconds to get his eyes used to the darkness inside, but couldn't afford to wait too long.

He wondered where the sheriff was. And others. Surely the number of shots would have been heard. If these men got away, he was going to make sure Sheriff Hastings lost his badge, if he had to tear it off his chest, himself.

Chapter Thirty-Four

He moved to the doorway, which had a curtain across it. That worked for him. He parted the curtain in the center and took a look. There was just enough moonlight for him to see two silhouettes in front of the window. He could also see that one held a rifle, and the other a pistol. But there were more shots than two men could have fired. That meant there were other men in other storefronts or, possibly, the roof.

If he could take these two, and keep one alive, that one could give up the others. Being taken alive, however, would be up to them.

He waited for a moment when both men were quiet, staring out the window, then stepped through the curtain, pointed his gun and cocked the hammer back. The two men froze.

"Keep still," Clint said. "I don't want to kill you."

"Jesus!" the man with the rifle yelled. "It's him!"

"Sonofabitch!" the other man growled. And started to bring his pistol around.

"He's gonna kill us," the first man said, starting to bring the rifle about.

"I'm not—" Clint started, but he had no time to talk to them. And in the dimness of the store, there was no time for any kind of trick shooting. He simply had to fire at the largest mass he could to stop them.

Since both men were standing, Clint was able to fire at them dead center. He actually heard the bullets strike their chests. They dropped their guns and fell lifeless to the floor.

"What the hell was that?" he heard somebody yell from somewhere—probably the other side of one of the walls.

"Zack you okay? Len?"

Zack and Len weren't okay. They were deed.

"Fine!" Clint shouted back, but he already knew it was too little too late.

"Let's get outta here!" somebody shouted, and he heard the sound of footsteps running out the front door and along the boardwalk.

He ran out the front of his store, which turned out to be some kind of clothing store. Once outside he heard someone running along the boardwalk, and someone else running down the street.

He holstered his gun and went back into the clothing store. He looked around, found a lamp, struck a Lucifer match and lit the wick. In the glow of the lamp he made sure the two men were dead, tossed their guns aside.

He knelt down and began to go through their pockets.

"Hold it right there!" someone said.

Clint turned and looked, saw Sheriff Hastings standing in the doorway with his gun in his hand.

"If you don't point that somewhere else you're going to regret it," Clint said.

"Adams? What the hell—"

"What's it look like?" Clint asked. "These two, and two or three others tried to bushwhack the hangman and me while we were across the street."

"In front of the leather store? It's a mess!"

"Yeah, well, we had to take cover somewhere." He continued to rifle through the dead men's pockets.

Hastings holstered his gun. "What're ya doin'?"

"Trying to find out who they are-or were."

"Any luck?"

"No." He stopped, stood. "Their pockets are empty. What about you? Know them?"

"Let me have a look."

Hastings came closer, leaned over and examined the faces of the two dead men. He hesitated, and Clint wondered if the man was considering lying.

"You know them," Clint said, to help him along.

"The big one's Zack Sadler"

"Does he work for Miklin?"

"Why would you ask that?"

"Come on, Hastings . . ."

"He did work for Miklin," the lawman said. "He don't, anymore."

"Since when? The ambush of Wainwright?"

"No, before that," Hastings said. "Before the kid got killed."

"Then why ambush the hangman?" Clint asked. "Why do this?"

"I don't know," Hastings said. "Maybe he thinks it'll get him back into the old man's good graces."

J.R. Roberts

"Isn't an attempt on the hangman's life enough reason to put off the hanging?"

"I can't make that decision."

"Why not?" Clint asked. "You've already delayed it once."

"I didn't delay nothin'," Hastings said. "You and the hangman did, with that business about the scale. What's next? A problem with the gallows?"

"Wainwright has already inspected it."

"The rope, then."

"Who knows?" Clint replied. "Where were you while all this shooting was going on?"

"The other end of town, doing my rounds," Hastings said. "When I got the word, I rushed right over. There were five, you said?"

"At least."

"Well, that leaves three," Hastings said. "Maybe I can find them."

"Like you found them the first time?" Clint asked.

The lawman ignored the remark.

"I'll get some men to clean up this mess," he said. "Why don't you go back to your hotel and get some rest? Tomorrow's a big day."

***

Clint knocked on Wainwright's door.

"Oh my God!" the hangman sad, when he saw him. "I thought you were dead."

136

"Not even close." He showed the man the bottle of whiskey he was carrying. "I stopped on the way here for this."

"Good," Wainwright said. "I need a drink."

Clint entered the room and closed the door behind him. There were no glasses so they sat on opposite sides of the bed and passed the bottle back and forth while Clint told him what had happened.

***

"I'm confused," Wainwright said, when they were halfway through the bottle.

"About what?"

Clint passed the bottle to the hangman.

"Sheriff Hastings," Wainwright said.

"What confuses you about him?" Clint asked. "He's pretty straightforward."

"If he knows who the bushwhackers were, why wouldn't he arrest them? I mean, if he's in favor of the prisoner hangin' he wouldn't want to leave them free to maybe kill me, right?"

"I don't know," Clint said, accepting the bottle back. "I don't know what's on that man's mind. I just know he's not a good lawman."

"Well, there's nothin' you can do about that, right?" Wainwright asked. "I mean, we'll both be leavin' after tomorrow, right?"

"That's right," Clint said. "After the hanging. There doesn't seem to be much more we can do to put it off. Unless . . ."

"Unless what?"

Clint hesitated, sipped from the bottle before saying, "This might just be the whiskey talking, but I could break him out tonight."

Chapter Thirty-Five

Planning to break a convicted murderer out of jail the night before he was to be executed was obviously a whiskey-soaked notion.

Clint left the hangman's room, leaving the inch or so of whiskey behind for the man to finish. Back in his own room he found himself thinking about breaking Dave Miklin out, again, and stowing him somewhere until he could clear him. But that was breaking the law, and while he may have done that a time or two—or more—in the past, it was always for a friend. Dave Miklin—and his father—were not his friends. They weren't even people he liked. And the same went for the distaff member of the family Belinda. Although he wouldn't have minded another go around with her in a hotel room, he would have liked to do it without her talking.

As for Wainwright, he'd only known the man slightly longer than he'd know the Miklins. And the hangman, himself, wasn't really sure he wanted the hanging stopped. He hadn't made his decision, yet, about possibly seeking a new profession.

So risking his own freedom, or his life, for that matter, didn't seem to be an option.

So what were his options?

***

Clint woke the next morning very upset with himself.

First, he had drunk too much whiskey the night before. His head hurt, and his mouth was dry as the desert.

Second, he'd gotten himself mixed up in a business that was none of his. Whether Wainwright continued with his profession as a hangman was of no concern of his. And whether or not Dave Miklin was hanged wasn't his business, either. A court of law had laid down the sentence.

Third, he couldn't help feeling that Sheriff Hastings needed to have his badge taken away from him. But what did it mean to him? Nothing!

Fourth, he still wanted to have sex again with Belinda Miklin. The other women he had already dallied with were nicer, but she was the one he was thinking—and dreaming—about. She was a coldhearted bitch, but in bed she was an inferno. He wondered if he could get her to sleep with him, but not talk while they were doing it?

And fifth, he couldn't remember what came fifth because of the first thing on his list, the goddamned drinking.

He got out of bed and doused his head with all the water in the pitcher on the dresser. Today was the day Dave Miklin was supposed to hang. Was there any chance the real killer would come forward to save him? Probably not.

In the end, after considering his options and his own reasons to keep out of it, Clint decided he had gone too far to give up now. He still had hours to work with—maybe more.

But first he needed breakfast, and a lot of coffee.

***

When Wainwright finally answered the door after several minutes of pounding on it, he looked disheveled and unhappy.

"My head hurt," he said. "What did we do last night?"

"We had a few drinks," Clint said. "And then I left the bottle with you and went to bed."

Wainwright looked behind him, then said, "I have an empty bottle here."

"That was it, I guess you finished it after I left."

Wainwright rubbed his face with both hands.

"I don't usually drink that much," he said.

"Well, I need something to eat, and a gallon of coffee. What about you?"

"I couldn't eat a thing," the hangman said. "Besides, I never eat on a morning that I'm . . . workin'."

"Okay," Clint said. "I'll stop back here after I'm done. Then we'll find out what time the sheriff expects you to hang his prisoner."

"Okay," Wainwright said. "Maybe my head will be hurtin' less by then."

Clint decided to stay in the hotel and have breakfast in their dining room.

As luck would have it, the Fate Inn did a perfectly cooked steak-and-egg breakfast, as well as a pot of very strong coffee.

Clint was enjoying both when the sheriff walked in and approached his table.

"I'm sorry to interrupt your breakfast, but we need to talk," the lawman said.

"Pull up a chair, Sheriff," Clint said, "and pour yourself a cup of coffee."

The lawman sat, but did not take the coffee.

"The mayor wants that boy hanged today," he said. "Within the hour, actually."

"Really? That quickly."

"Where's the hangman?"

"He's in his room, trying to recover from the effects of sharing a bottle of whiskey with me last night. Neither of us is used to that kind of drinking."

"Is that a fact?" Hastings said. "The legendary Gunsmith has a hangover?"

"Beer is my normal drink, Sheriff," Clint said. "I'm not real fond of whiskey."

"Well," Hastings said, "I need Wainwright over at the jail as soon as possible." The man seemed to be growing more and more agitated by the moment.

"Last night he said he only needed to check his rope."

"We got a rope on the gallows," Hastings said. "The mayor is on my ass, Adams. So I'm on yours."

"A hangman uses his own rope, Sheriff," Clint said. "You ought to know that."

"Well," Hastings said, standing up, "get him and his rope over to the jail this morning!"

"Got it, Sheriff," Clint said. "As soon as I finish my breakfast."

"You better hurry!" Hastings snapped. "My job might be on the line, here."

He turned and stormed out of the room. Clint immediately had second thoughts about Hastings being the killer. He seemed very afraid of losing his $30 a month job, which seemed reason enough to want Miklin to hang. It was the mayor who was putting on the pressure.

And Clint hadn't spoken with the mayor, yet.

***

"What, now?"

"Immediately, he said," Clint replied to the hangman.

"I'm still feelin' poorly," Wainwright said.

"Then you need something to eat."

"No, I told you," the man said, "not before a hangin'."

"Then maybe," Clint said, "what you need is some hair of the dog.

Chapter Thirty-Six

They managed to scare up a bottle of whiskey from the kitchen.

"I'll pay you for the bottle," Clint told the waiter, "but we only need one drink."

"Yessir," the waiter said.

Clint took the bottle, poured about a finger or two into a glass, and handed it to Wainwright.

"You sure?" the hangman asked.

"Pick you right up."

Wainwright took it and drank it down.

"All right," Clint said, taking the empty glass and handing it to the waiter, who was still holding the bottle. "Thanks for that."

"Anytime, sir."

"Carl, let's go and get your rope."

***

They went from the hotel to the livery stable and Clint waited outside while Wainwright went into his wagon. For the first time he noticed what was written on the back door of the wagon. Actually, it was scrawled, but legibly. It said: PROFESSIONAL HANGMAN, and beneath that in smaller print BEST RATES IN THE BUSINESS.

Wainwright came out with the rope and Clint pointed to the door.

"Is that true?"

"I hope it is," the hangman said. "It's also written on the side."

"I guess I didn't stop to read," Clint said.

"This rope is very sturdy," Wainwright said. "So what do we do now?"

"That's easy," Clint said. "We cut it."

***

"This has been cut!" Sheriff Hastings said

"Sorry? What?" Clint asked.

Hastings held the rope out in front of him, having just snatched it from Wainwright's hand.

"It's been cut by a knife."

"Uh, no," Wainwright said, "there's a bin in the back of my wagon that has a pretty sharp edge on it. The rope must have rubbed against it during the trip here."

"Against the edge of a bin?"

"Well, it was in the bin, only this part," Wainwright said, touching the rope where Clint had just recently cut it, "was hangin' over—"

"Okay," Hastings said, throwing the rope back to Wainwright, "go and get a new rope."

"It ain't that easy," Wainwright said. "I gotta get it, then test it."

"How long will that take?" the sheriff asked.

"A few hours."

"I guess I'll have to tell the mayor."

"I'll go with you," Clint said, "I'd like to meet the man who has you so jittery."

"I ain't jittery!" Hastings claimed. "I just don't wanna lose my job." He pointed a finger at Wainwright. "You go and get a rope!"

"Alone?"

Clint put his hand on the man's shoulder.

"We'll take you over there," Clint said. "Then you can stay in the livery and test it while we talk to the mayor." He looked at Hastings. "That play with you, Sheriff?"

"That's fine," Hastings said. "Let's just do it!"

Chapter Thirty-Seven

Wainwright found a likely rope at Fate's general store, and then Clint and Hastings walked him over to the livery stable.

"Sam?" Hastings called out.

Sam Holcroft came out of the back room.

"What's goin' on, Sheriff?"

"Mr. Wainwright has to stay here and test this new rope," the sheriff said. "I need somebody to look out for him, make sure nobody shoots him. If they do we won't have a hangin'."

"Well, just let me get my rifle, then," Holcroft said, "and I'll look after 'im."

"Thanks, Sam. Mr. Adams and me, we gotta go talk to the mayor."

"Well, you give hizzoner my best," Holcroft said, "and tell 'im I hope he chokes to death on his next meal."

He cackled and went in the back to get his rifle.

"Doesn't sound like Mr. Holcroft has much use for the mayor," Clint said.

"Hates him," Hastings said.

"And when I came to town he told me he didn't like Henry Miklin, either."

"Sam has a little problem with authority."

"He seems to get along with you," Clint commented.

"I don't wave my authority in people's faces," Hastings replied.

Holcroft came back out with his rifle, a Winchester 1866 "Yellow Boy," and Hastings turned to Wainwright.

"Get that rope ready!" he snapped.

"I'll do my best."

***

Clint followed Sheriff Hastings to the Fate City Hall. It was a one story building that looked as if it had once been a store of some kind. Clint wondered why the mayor didn't rate a new building?

"Not much of a City Hall," Clint observed, when they stepped inside.

"We're havin' one built," Hastings said, then added, "if we have the money that is."

"And that depends on Henry Miklin?"

"Right."

"Odd, then, that the mayor wants this hanging to take place so badly."

"He just wants to get it over with so he can deal with the backlash," Hastings said.

Hastings knocked and they entered the mayor's office. Clint disliked politicians almost as much as he disliked wealthy, arrogant ranchers. So here he was, getting himself involved with both.

"Mayor, this is Clint Adams," Hastings said. "Adams, Mayor Fletcher."

Fletcher was a full figure of a man in his 50s—not fat, but he seemed to fill the room with his bulk. He did not come around the desk, and did not offer to shake hands.

"What the hell is going on, Adams?" he demanded.

"Nice to meet you too, Mayor."

"I don't have time for pleasantries," the man said. "I have to do damage control to keep Henry Miklin from dropping this town into the latrine. But first we have to get past this hanging."

"I have no control over the problems the hangman seems to be having—"

"Don't give me that horseshit," the mayor said, cutting him off. "What the hell is going on?"

"Well," Clint said, "I don't happen to think the boy is guilty."

"Can you prove it?" the mayor asked. "Can you point out the guilty party?"

"Right at this moment, no," Clint said. "But I have some ideas."

"We don't have time for your ideas!"

"Don't have time to make sure you don't hang an innocent man?" Clint asked.

"The judge and jury—"

"—I know, have spoken," Clint said. "That's what I've been hearing. But they can be wrong. It's happened before."

"Mr. Adams," the mayor said, "you're asking us to believe you, a man with a reputation as a gunman and killer, over the legal decision of a court. You want me to put my career as a politician on the line?"

"I'm confused," Clint said. "Wouldn't hanging Henry Miklin's son, if he's innocent, hurt your career as a politician?"

"It's not my decision," Fletcher said, "it's the court's decision."

"I see."

"I don't really care if you see or not," the mayor said. He looked at Hastings. "Get it done today! The whole town is waiting."

"Yessir."

"That's all." He sat back down and ignored both men.

Hastings and Clint left the building, stopped just outside.

"What are these ideas you have?" the sheriff asked.

"Well," Clint said, "one was you."

"Me? Are you crazy?"

"No," Clint said, "at the time I was drunk."

"You musta been! Why me?"

"You seemed to be in a hurry to get the boy hung."

"Because the mayor's on my ass."

"I get that now," Clint said. "What about the mayor?"

"What about him?"

"Does he have any reason to want the Miklin boy dead? Is he out for revenge against the old man?"

"That old man is Fletcher's ticket to the governor's mansion," Hastings said. "He tried to influence the judge, but it was no use. Since he was a circuit judge, and didn't live here, he stuck to his guns. He thought Miklin was guilty, and so did the jury."

"If I had time I'd talk to each jury member," Clint said. "But time is the one thing we don't have a lot of."

"You and that hangman have held it up as long as you can," Hastings said "It's gonna happen."

Clint noticed that people on the street were all turning their attention in the same direction.

"What's going on?" he said, aloud.

They both looked up the street and saw what was attracting everyone's attention. Henry Miklin was riding into town with a bunch of his men.

"Miklin told me he was looking for legal means to save his son," Clint said.

"Maybe," Sheriff Hastings said, "he changed his mind."

Clint and Hastings both stepped into the street as Miklin approached.

"You hang my boy yet, Sheriff?" Miklin asked, reining in.

"No, sir," Hastings said, "It ain't my job. But the hangman's gettin' ready to do it today."

"And you, Adams," the rancher said, "you haven't proved Dave innocent yet, have you?"

"I haven't," Clint said, "I think he's innocent, but I haven't proved it."

"That's it, then," Miklin said. "The boy's definitely going to hang."

"Looks like it, Mr. Miklin," Hastings said. "I'm real sorry, but that's the law. I'm only doing my job."

"And Sheriff," Miklin said, "just remember that when the time comes, I'll be doing my job as a father."

He rode on, followed by his foreman.

Hastings turned to Clint and looking puzzled, asked, "What job?"

"I guess that's something we're going to find out."

Chapter Thirty-Eight

After Miklin and his men had ridden away Clint turned to the sheriff.

"I have an idea."

"Another way to delay the hangin'?"

"No," Clint said, "but I think we should ask Mr. Miklin to take a look at the bodies of the two men I killed."

"I told you Zack worked for him."

"I want to see his reaction," Clint said. "And maybe he knows the other man, and the men who were also shooting at us."

"All right," Hastings said. "They probably went to the Lodge. Let's go over and see if we can catch him there."

"It's early—"

"It'll open for him," Hastings assured Clint. "He owns it."

***

When they reached the Lodge Saloon, Miklin's and his men's horses were tied outside. As they entered they saw all the men at the bar.

Miklin turned, holding a beer, and saw them approaching him.

"Now what?" he asked.

"We need you to make an identification," Sheriff Hastings said.

"Of who?"

"That's the question," Clint said. "The bushwhackers tried again last night to kill the hangman. I killed two of them. I want to find out if you knew them. And if you did, you might be able to guess who the others were."

"Very well," Miklin said. "Where are they?"

"The undertaker's," Hastings said.

"I'll finish this beer and meet you there," Miklin said. "Say half an hour?"

"Fine," Hastings said, before Clint could object.

"And I'll bring Bill with me," he said, gesturing toward his foreman. "He might know them."

"Okay," Clint said, "but don't be late. This might go toward proving your son innocent."

"Is that right?" Miklin said, raising his eyebrows. "Then I'll be there in fifteen minutes."

***

Clint and Hastings went to the undertaker to make sure he would be open when Miklin got there. The small, middle-aged man, whose name was Tischel, let them in and showed them where the bodies were.

"I've got to go out to pick up a body," he said. "All right if I leave you here?"

"That's fine," Hastings said.

"I'll be back as soon as I can."

"Any problem?" Hastings asked.

"No," Tischel said. "Mrs. Clune finally passed. She was ninety-six."

"You don't need me, then."

"No."

"Good."

Tischel left, leaving Clint and Hastings alone.

"Do you usually get involved when somebody dies of natural causes?" Clint asked.

"Not if it *was* natural causes," Hastings said. "I just have to make sure. It's my job."

"Which you might be better at than I thought."

"Well . . . thanks."

"I'm sorry," Clint said, "I just thought . . . well, with you seeming to be in an all fired hurry to hang Miklin . . ."

"Forget it," the sheriff said. "I know I'm good at my job, which is what counts."

"I suppose you're right."

Moments later Henry Miklin arrived with his foreman, Bill Cameron.

"Let's have a look at these bodies," he said.

Clint and Hastings took the two men to the back to show them. Clint watched them both closely as Hastings uncovered each dead man.

"I don't know them," Miklin said.

"That one is Zack Sadler," the lawman said, pointing. "He used to work for you."

"I don't know every man who works for me," Miklin commented.

"He does," Clint said, indicating the foreman.

"Come on, Cameron," Hastings said. "You know these two?"

"Yeah, I knew Zack," Cameron said. "I fired him last month, and that's Roscoe Pennell." He looked at his boss. "He works for us."

"Then what was he doing in town last night shooting at Adams and the hangman?" Miklin asked.

"I don't know, boss," Cameron said. "I knew he was in town, but not what he was doin'."

"There were two or three other men with them," Clint said. "Who would they be?"

"I—I don't know," Cameron said.

"Who else was in town?" Clint asked.

Cameron didn't reply immediately.

"Well, come on, man," Miklin said, "answer the question!"

"Lon Mckee, Ben Bagby and Shorty Daniels. They're all friends."

"Well," Miklin said, "they're all fired, and I might even fire you. Are you sure you didn't know about this? And ambushing the hangman outside of town?"

"I had no idea boss. I swear."

Clint watched the interchange between the two men. It was his opinion they were both being truthful.

"I'm sorry about this, Adams," Miklin said.

"Not your fault, Mr. Miklin," Clint said, "but why are you in town today?"

"Not to try and stop the hanging by force, is it?" Sheriff Hastings asked.

"No, Sheriff," Miklin said, "but I am here to see my boy one more time before you stretch his neck."

"Of course."

"Cameron," Clint said, "where are those other three men you mentioned."

Cameron looked nervous.

"Well?" Miklin demanded.

"They're in the saloon," Cameron said. "They rode in with us."

"Jesus, Mary and Joseph!" Miklin swore. "You *are* fired, Cameron!"

Chapter Thirty-Nine

The four men went from the undertaker back to the Lodge Saloon, where the three ranch hands in question were laughing and drinking.

"Let's go," the sheriff said. "You three are under arrest."

"What for?" Shorty Daniels asked.

"Drinkin' too early," Hastings said, "before opening time."

"What?" Bagby asked, laughing. "They're open."

"No," Miklin said. "we're not."

"Hey, boss—" McKee started.

"I'm not your boss anymore," Miklin said. "You're all fired."

"What?" Bagby asked.

"Boss—" Mckee started to say to Cameron, but the other man cut him off.

"I ain't your boss anymore," Cameron said. "I got fired, too."

"Come on, let's go," Hastings said. "I'll take your guns." He grabbed their guns from their holsters as they walked past him.

"You comin'?" the lawman asked Clint.

"I'll be along," Clint said. "Just find out if they were working for somebody or just being stupid."

"Could be both," Hastings said and left.

Miklin walked to the front doors, looked at Cameron and said, "Get out. You might as well go back to the ranch and clean out your gear."

"Boss, can't we talk—"

"No!"

Cameron left. Miklin closed the doors and locked them.

"Set 'em up," he said to the bartender.

The bartender put two fresh beers on the bar.

"Go ahead," Miklin said, "if Hastings tries to arrest you, too, I'll tell him we're open."

Clint picked up the beer.

"So what've you got?" Miklin asked.

"Well, now I know who ambushed the hangman," Clint said. "This Zack might've been trying to get his job back by keeping your son from hanging."

"By killing the hangman?" Miklin shook his head. "They just would've gotten another one."

"Right, but he was too dumb to figure that out."

"Then he wouldn't have got his job back," Miklin said. "What about my son? Do you have anything?"

"I thought I did, but it turned out to be wrong. What about the mayor?"

"What about him?"

"Are you friends with him?"

"No."

"Are you a supporter of his?"

"As mayor? Or as a politician?"

"Either one."

"Well, as mayor of Fate, maybe. As a politician with his eyes on the governor's house? No."

"Does he know that?"

"I don't know?"

"If he did would he take revenge by framing your son for murder and then hanging him?"

Miklin stared at Clint for a few moments, considering, then said, "Nah, he don't have the gumption for that."

"No," Clint said, "from my one meeting with him, I don't think so, either."

"So nobody else?"

"I'm afraid not."

Miklin finished his beer.

"You going over to the sheriff's office?" he asked.

"I told him I would."

"I'll come with you," the rancher said. "I want to see my boy."

Clint finished his beer, and they left the Lodge.

Chapter Forty

As Clint and Henry Miklin entered the sheriff's office, they interrupted the racket that was going on. The three ex-ranch hands were shouting, and Clint couldn't tell if they were yelling at the sheriff, or among themselves. The lawman, for his part, was sitting back in his chair, watching and listening. When he saw Clint and Miklin he stood up and walked over.

"What's going on?" Miklin asked.

"They're tryin' to figure out who's gonna tell me the truth," Hastings said.

"Well, I'd like to see my boy."

"Sure," the sheriff said. "Come this way."

Miklin followed Hastings into the cell block, and Clint remained in the office. But rather than watch them argue, he decided to take part.

"Shut up, the three of you!" he shouted.

They all fell silent and looked at him.

"Who recruited you to ambush the hangman?" They all looked at each other. "Don't make me ask again. The three of you shot at me, too, and I don't take kindly to that."

"It was Zack," one of them said.

"Who are you?"

"McKee," the man said. "Zack got fired. He said if he saved Dave then he'd get his job back. We agreed to help."

"Why?"

"He's our friend."

"So you agreed to kill a man because a friend asked you to?" Clint asked. "That makes no sense."

The three men looked at each other again.

"Come on, come on!" Clint said. "Make sense."

"He said he'd pay us!" another man said.

"Which one are you?"

"Bagby."

"How much did he offer you?"

"A lot," Bagby said.

"Where was he going to get the money to pay you?" Clint asked.

The third man, who he assumed was Shorty Daniels, even though he was tall and thin, said, "Miklin."

"Henry Miklin hired him?"

"No," McKee said, "not Henry."

"Belinda?" Clint asked. Surprised.

"No."

"That only leaves . . .

". . . Dave."

Chapter Forty-One

Hastings came out of the cell block.

"I need to speak to Dave Miklin," Clint said.

"Go on through, then," Hastings said. "I'm gonna get rid of these three or lock them up."

"Don't lock them up," Clint said.

"Why not?"

"Because Dave Miklin hired them," Clint said. "They shouldn't be in a cell block with him."

"The kid hired them?"

"Well, he hired Zack Sadler and Sadler hired them," Clint said.

"So what do I do with them?"

"I don't know," Clint said. "Let me talk to Miklin."

Clint went into the cell block. Henry Miklin was standing in front of his son's cell, facing him and berating him.

". . . . finally going to have to pay for being stupid."

"You don't know how stupid," Clint said.

Both of the Miklins turned to look at him.

"What do you mean?" Henry asked.

"Do you want to tell your father, or should I?" Clint asked Dave.

"Tell me what?" Henry asked. He looked at Clint, then at Dave. "What's he talking about?"

Dave turned and sat down on his cot.

"It was Dave who sent Zack Sadler and those other men after the hangman," Clint said.

"What?" He looked at his son. "Stupid!"

"Yeah, you're always tellin' me that," Dave said.

"What were you thinking?" Henry asked.

"I was thinkin' I don't wanna hang for somerhin' I didn't do!"

"So you still maintain your innocence?" Clint asked.

"Yeah, I do," Dave said. "I thought you believed me."

"I did, until I found out you sent some men to kill the hangman."

"I never told Zack to kill 'im!" Dave snapped. "I told him I'd pay him to scare him away."

"And what about the ambush on the street?" Clint asked. "They tried to kill the hangman and me."

"I don't know anythin' about that," Dave said. "Zack musta did that on his own, and got killed for it."

"Dave didn't kill that Tillman boy," Henry said. "I'm sure of it. But that's no excuse for what he did."

"No, it's not," Clint agreed. "Who's got it in for you, Mr. Miklin? Who hates you enough to have killed Roy Tillman and framed Dave?"

"Who knows?" Miklin said. "Anybody I've done business with."

"Which is most of the town, isn't it?"

"Yes."

"All right." Clint looked at Dave. "The sheriff might be arresting McKee, Bagby and Daniels. If he puts them in the cell next to you, don't talk to them. Anything else you do could hurt any chance of proving you innocent."

"What's it matter?" Dave asked. "I'm gonna hang today."

"Just do what the Gunsmith tells you," Henry said. "Don't be—"

"—I know," Dave said. "Stupid!"

***

Clint and Henry Miklin came out from the cell block.

"Go ahead and lock them up, Sheriff," Clint said.

"Are you sure? What about Dave?"

"He won't talk to them," Henry said.

"Well, it doesn't really matter, does it?" Hastings said. "I mean—"

"I know what you mean," Miklin said. "I'll be staying in town so I can take my boy home when you release him."

"Mr. Miklin—"

Miklin left the office.

"Why does he think—"

"He's hoping."

"Even if you proved him innocent I couldn't just let him go without the judge—

"Let's worry about that later, Sheriff," Clint said. "Why don't you lock these three up."

"Right."

"I'm going to check on Wainwright," Clint said, and left the office.

***

As Clint entered the livery stable there was a single shot. The bullet imbedded itself into the wall next to him.

"Hold on!" he shouted. "It's me."

"Sorry, sorry," Sam Holcroft shouted. He and Wainwright came out from hiding. "This hangman's makin' me a nervous mess."

"I can't help it," the hangman said. "I'm jumpin' at shadows."

"Well, you don't have to, anymore," Clint said. "The rest of the men that bushwhacked you are in jail."

"Really?"

"In a cell right next to young Miklin."

"So . . . I'm safe. Nobody wants to kill me? Or stop me?" Wainwright asked.

"Well," Clint said, "nobody wants to kill you, but Henry Miklin would still like to stop you from hanging his son."

"Who were those men workin' for?" Wainwright asked.

"Turns out we had the right idea, but the wrong Miklin," Clint said. "Dave promised them money if they kept him from hanging."

Sam Holcroft cackled.

"That fool boy. Is he still gonna hang?"

"Probably," Clint said.

Holcroft slapped Wainwright on the back.

"Then you still get to do your work, hangman," He said, "and I'll be there to watch." The old man looked very happy.

"And so will a lot of people," Clint said. "How's your rope, Carl."

"Uh, the rope is, uh . . . fine?"

"The sheriff is waiting to hear that," Clint said. "But don't think it matters."

"Why's that?" Wainwright asked.

"Because I think maybe I can save him, even if it's at the last minute."

"Even if he's guilty?" Holcroft asked.

"He's not," Clint said, "and I'm going to prove it, hopefully in time." He waved to Wainwright. "Come on. Bring your rope."

They left the livery, leaving Sam Holcroft behind.

Chapter Forty-Two

"Henry Miklin is staying in town," Clint said, as they walked back to the sheriff's office.

"Why would he do that?" Wainwright asked. "Why would he watch his son hang?"

"I think he still believes that I'll save him."

"And do you believe that?" Wainwright asked.

"I believe that I'll keep trying," Clint said, "and I'm not even sure why."

"The money?"

"No," Clint said, "I already said I'm not in it for the money."

"So who do you think killed the other boy, if not Dave Miklin?"

"It was someone who hates Henry Miklin, not somebody who hated Roy Tillman."

"So the dead boy was just a pawn?"

"Yes."

"That's too bad."

"Yes, it is."

They reached the sheriff's office and entered. It was much quieter than it had been when Clint left.

"Sheriff," Wainwright said, and held out his rope.

"It's ready?" the lawman asked.

"It is," the hangman said, "I just have to get it to the gallows and test it there."

"How long will that take?" Hastings asked.

"Not lo—I, uh, we'll have to see."

"Well, get it done," the sheriff said.

"Is Dave keeping his mouth shut?" Clint asked.

"So far."

"Then I'll walk over to the gallows with Carl and watch."

"He's in no danger, anymore," Hastings said, "not with those three locked up and the other two dead."

"Just the same . . ."

"Yeah," Hastings said, "might as well be safe."

The office door opened and the mayor walked in.

"Sheriff, we need to talk!"

"Yes, Mr. Mayor," Hastings said. "This is our hangman, Mr. Wainwright."

The mayor turned and looked at the hangman.

"So, you're ready, then?"

"Just about," Wainwright said.

"We're just going to the gallows to test the rope," Clint said.

"It looks fine to me," the mayor said.

"Like Clint said, we're gonna test it."

"We're leaving now," Clint said.

"Just as well," the mayor said, and turned toward the sheriff.

Clint and Wainwright went outside and started walking toward the gallows.

"He seems to want this to happen quickly," the hangman said.

169

"Supposedly, just so he can deal with the aftermath," Clint said. "He's going to try to convince Henry Miklin not to leave town."

"After they kill his son?" Wainwright shook his head. "I haven't spent time with the man, but it seems to me that doesn't seem likely. In fact, I'd think he'd want to burn the town to the ground."

"Yes," Clint said, "I'd think that, too. But he does seem to want to clear his son legally. Even after the boys hangs I don't know if he'd go the other way and do something illegal. I mean, if he won't break the law to save his son, why break it to avenge him?"

"That all makes sense," Wainwright said, "except that nothin' about this makes sense. Including the way I'm feelin'."

"One way or another this is going to end today," Clint said, "and then you can make your final decision about what you want to do."

As they approached the gallows Wainwright said, "I hope you're right."

Chapter Forty-Three

Clint watched as Wainwright walked up the steps and hooked the rope. He needed Clint's help to use a body-sized sandbag that was already there to test its strength. Clint climbed the steps and together they hooked up the bag and dropped it through the trap door. But just before they did that there was a shot. The bullet struck the sandbag just as the trap door opened. Clint and Wainwright dropped to their bellies, and it got so quiet that they could hear the sand sifting from the bag through the hole.

"What the hell—" Wainwright said. "I thought all the bushwhackers were accounted for?"

"They are," Clint said.

"Then who fired that shot?" Wainwright asked.

"I don't know," Clint said, "but I'm going to find out. Come on, let's get down from here."

***

There wasn't another shot, so they had time to collect the partially empty sandbag and, right beneath the gallows, dig through it for the bullet, which Clint was holding in his hand as Sheriff Hastings made his appearance.

"What happened?" He joined them beneath the gallows.

"Somebody took a shot at me," Wainwright said.

"Well," Clint said, "A shot at one of us. With this." He held the bullet up between his thumb and forefinger.

"A forty-four?" Hastings said.

Clint nodded.

"Did anyone take the bullet that killed Roy Tillman out of his body?" Clint asked.

Hastings nodded. "The doc."

"Where is it?"

"He probably still has it."

"It wasn't presented in court?"

"No."

"Why not?"

"The judge didn't want it. he said we didn't have an 'expert' in town to comment on it."

"Well," Clint said, "you've got an expert now."

***

Sheriff Hastings took Clint and Wainwright to the office of Doctor Barnaby.

"Why yes," Barnaby, a well-seasoned sawbones in his 60s, said, "I kept the bullet. I don't know why, actually."

"Could you find it now, Doc?" Clint asked.

"I suppose so," Barnaby said. "Let me take a look."

As the doctor left the room Hastings looked at Clint and asked, "What are you gonna do with the bullet?"

Clint took out the other one and said, "Compare it to this one."

"And then?"

"Find the gun, find the shooter."

"What are you gonna do, use a magnifyin' glass? You gonna use this, whatayacallit, ballistics thing? You a scientist, now?"

Clint was surprised Hastings knew anything about ballistics.

"No," Clint said, but I'm a gunsmith. I'm just going to take a look at the two bullets, and compare them. For instance, see these two marks?"

He held the bullet so the sheriff could see where the hammer had struck.

"This bullet was fired by a gun with two firing pins," Clint said.

"What kinda gun would that be?"

"Could be an old Henry, or an early Winchester," Clint said. "If the other bullet has the same marks, I'll have some idea what to look for."

The doctor came back and said, "You're in luck. Here it is." He handed it to Clint. "You're lucky there's not much damage to it. Sometimes bullets just fragment inside the body. Now, if you don't mind, I've got some patients to see."

Clint and the sheriff stepped outside, where Clint held both bullets, one in each hand, so he could examine them in the sunlight.

"See?" he said to the sheriff. "The same marks. Chances are these bullets were fired from the same gun."

"There's gotta be more than one gun in town with two firin' pins," Hastings said.

"Now that I know what I'm looking for," Clint said, "I'll be able to find out."

"That may be so," Hastings said, "but you won't have the time."

"Did you announce the hangings?"

'The mayor made me put out the word that Miklin will be hung at three."

"What's that give me, three hours?"

"Just about."

"I guess that'll have to be enough."

Chapter Forty-Four

Clint needed someplace quiet to think, so he asked if he could go back to the sheriff's office with him.

"Why not?" Hastings said. "I've got to wait there with the prisoner."

When they got there, Wainwright was sitting in a chair in front of the sheriff's desk.

"What are you doin' here?"

"I didn't know where else to wait," he said. "People are already gatherin' out there."

"Yeah, we saw them," Hastings said, sitting behind his desk. "They bein' quiet in there?" He jerked his head toward the cell block.

"Not a word since I've been here." He looked at Clint. "What've you got?"

Clint held up his hand. "Two bullets, the one that killed Tillman and the one fired at us."

"At me, you mean."

"I've been thinking about that," Clint said. "I think the bullet struck closer to me than to you."

"Why would someone want to shoot you?" Hastings asked. "If they want to stop the hangin' they'd shoot Mr. Wainwright," He looked at the hangman. "Sorry."

"Don't be. That's what I was thinkin'."

"Well, here's what I'm thinking," Clint said. "Maybe they didn't want to kill you to stop the hanging. Instead, maybe they wanted to kill me to make sure it went ahead. I mean, since I'm the one trying to stop it."

"That's an idea," Hastings said. "So that would make Wainwright safe."

"Pretty much."

"So he can hang Dave Miklin at three."

"If he has to."

"You still think you can stop it?"

"I need to play some things back in my head," Clint said, "but I think I have an idea who killed Tillman."

"Who?" Hastings asked. "Who do you suspect."

"I'm not going to say," Clint said. "I told you, I need to mull some things over."

"Well, mull fast," the lawman said.

"I will."

Clint sat in a chair by the window.

"It ain't me, is it?" Hastings asked.

Clint didn't answer.

Chapter Forty-Five

The three ex-ranch hands in their cell started to make noise at one point about being hungry, but Hastings went in and shut them up.

Wainwright stood up, walked over to stand by Clint and looked out the window at the gathering crowd. As in many cases before, the sheriff would have to walk the prisoners completely through the crowd to get to the gallows. Wainwright himself would already be there, waiting for them.

The hangman looked at Clint wanting to say something but seeing that he was deep in thought he walked back to his chair in front of the sheriff's desk and sat back down.

"Goddamnit!" Clint said, at that point, and sprang to his feet.

"What is it?" Wainwright asked.

"You got it?" Hastings said.

"I think I do."

"You got an hour to spare," the lawman said. "Whataya gonna do?"

"I'll be back," Clint said, heading for the door.

"You want me to come with ya?" Hastings asked.

"No," Clint said, "if I don't make it back, you and Carl will have to do your jobs."

He opened the door and ran out, slamming it behind him.

Outside Clint had to push his way through the crowd, all shouting at him, asking when the hanging was going to take place. Finally, once he got past the gallows, the crowd thinned. Across the street he saw the mayor standing in front of a café, drinking a cup of coffee. He walked over.

"Waiting for the hanging?" he asked.

"I am," the mayor said. "I just don't like crowds."

"You have the authority to call it off, don't you?" Clint asked. "In the absence of a judge?"

"I suppose—"

"Well, be ready to act fast," Clint said. "You may be the only thing standing between an innocent man and a rope."

"Believe me," the mayor said, "if you can prove he didn't do it, I'll be happy to step in. I'm really not looking forward to hanging the son of the most powerful man in town."

Clint turned and hurried away from the mayor. He had wasted enough time, already. But along the way he saw another man standing on the boardwalk, waiting. This one was in front of the Lodge Saloon, holding a beer.

Henry Miklin.

The man obviously also had no desire to stand in amongst the crowd. Clint decided not to stop to speak to him.

Something had been niggling at the back of Clint's brain since the shooting of the gallows dummy. Sitting in the sheriff's office, trying to quiet his mind so that it would come to the forefront, worked as it finally materialized.

The shot.

The sound of the shot combined with the bullets bearing the marks of the double firing pin. That's when he knew what rifle had been used. And he had seen one in town. Of course, there could have been more than one, but that would be a hell of a coincidence—and Clint Adams didn't like or believe in coincidences.

When he reached the livery he went in, found it empty.

"Sam?"

No answer.

"Come on, Holcroft, I know you're here."

After a moment the old man's voice came from the back.

"That boy's neck stretched yet?"

"Not yet."

"Then you better get it done."

"I know that's what you want, Sam," Clint said, "but it's not going to happen."

"Why not?" He sounded disappointed.

"Because of that rifle I'm sure you're pointing at me right now."

Holcroft came from the shadows in the back and, sure enough, he was holding his rife on Clint.

"What about my rifle?"

"You used it to shoot at me just a little while ago," Clint said. "It's a Winchester Yellow Boy. Not too many of those around town, I bet."

"How do you know what it was?"

"I could tell by the sound," Clint said. "See, if I'm an expert on anything it's guns. You used that Yellow Boy to shoot at me, and you used it to kill Roy Tillman."

"You can't prove nothin'."

179

"Actually, I can," Clint said, "because I've got both bullets. They match each other, and I'm sure they'll match the bullets in your rifle."

Holcroft frowned, flexed his fingers on his rifle, as if it was getting heavier.

"Why would I kill that boy?" Holcroft demanded. "I didn't even know 'im."

"Yeah, you did. You bought him whiskey, and egged him on to start a fight with Dave Miklin. Then later you killed him, knowing Miklin would get the blame."

"Why would I do that?"

"You told me when I first rode in how Henry Miklin was trying to buy you out. You said you hated him, and hoped his boy would hang. But you didn't just hope it. You were trying to make it happen."

"I wasn't tryin' ta kill the hangman," Holcroft said. "That was somebody else."

"Yeah, we figured that part out," Clint said, "but you did try to kill me a few hours ago. You figured if I was dead, nobody was going to try to prove Dave innocent and he'd hang. Only you're not such a good shot, are you, Sam?"

Suddenly, Sam cackled and said, "Good enough to put one in that boy's back."

"Oh sure, in an empty lot," Clint said.

"Good enough to put one in your belly right now."

"Why do that?" Clint asked. "All you've got to do is hold me here until the hanging is over."

"And then I go to jail," Holcroft said. "That ain't gonna work for me. So now yer gonna gimme those two bullets, and then I'm gonna kill ya."

"They're in my pocket, Sam. You're going to have to come over here and get them."

"I ain't that stupid," Sam said. "So I'll kill ya first, and then get the bullets outta yer pocket."

"Then you better do it fast because I'm about to draw and fire and kill you, Sam."

"You can't," Sam said. "I got the rifle pointing dead atcha."

"But you forget who I am," Clint said.

"The goddamn Gunsmith!" Sam Holcroft said. "Why'd you hafta ruin my plan? I figured if Miklin's son hung he'd leave this town and I'd get to keep my place. Well, that's what's gonna happen."

"I don't think so, Sam."

Clint was pretty sure he could draw before the man fired, but there always the chance he'd catch a bullet in the process. Turned out in didn't matter, because they were both surprised by the sound of a shot, and then blood blossomed on the man's chest. His eyes wide, he dropped the rifle, and then dropped down onto it, face down.

Dead.

Clint looked over at the door of the stable, saw Henry Miklin standing there with a gun in his hand.

"Sonofabitch!" he swore. "I don't even know this man!"

Clint checked Sam to make sure he was dead, then turned to Miklin.

"He says he knew you. You were trying to buy his business."

"That was my lawyer," Miklin said. "I never met this man, and he wanted to make my son hang."

"Well," Clint said, "we're going to have to move and talk fast if we're going to keep that from happening."

"Jesus!" Miklin said.

They both started running.

Chapter Forty-Six

The next day the townspeople gathered round the gallows. But it wasn't to see a hanging, it was to see it burn.

It had taken a lot of talking on the part of Clint and Henry Miklin the day before, but the mayor finally called off the hanging, even before Sheriff Hastings had a chance to take Dave out of his cell. And, as he had planned, Henry Miklin got to take his boy home—although he was berating him all the way.

Miklin offered to pay Clint the money he had offered in the beginning, but Clint turned it down. He was satisfied to have kept an innocent boy from hanging, and Carl Wainwright from getting killed.

It was all over.

***

Clint and the hangman decided to leave the next morning. However, they were going separate ways, since Wainwright no longer needed protection.

Clint had spent the night alone. Among the three women he had spent time with in Fate, he would have liked a return engagement with Belinda Miklin, but he just couldn't bring himself to spend time with someone who had such a horrible personality, no matter how good the sex was.

He and Wainwright had breakfast together in the Fate Inn. They didn't talk much, rather each of them was alone with his own thoughts about what they had gone through. When they went out front Eclipse was saddled and ready, standing next to Wainwright's wagon.

"Have you made a decision about what you're going to do next, Carl?" Clint asked Wainwright, as the man climbed aboard his wagon.

"No, but thanks to you, I now have the time to think it over," the man said. If I do change professions, though, I'd have to get my entire wagon repainted.

Clint mounted up and, on even footing, they shook hands and said goodbye. Wainwright's wagon went one way, and Clint went the other. He was thinking if the prospect of painting his wagon was enough to keep Carl Wainwright from changing his profession then his bad dreams would probably fade. Then he would continue to ply his trade as an executioner—perhaps a reluctant one, but a hangman, nevertheless.

After the experience with an innocent man almost being hanged, Clint had no desire to be a hangman, know another hangman, or ever attend another hanging.

Coming July 27, 2018

THE GUNSMITH
438
The Treasure of Little Bighorn

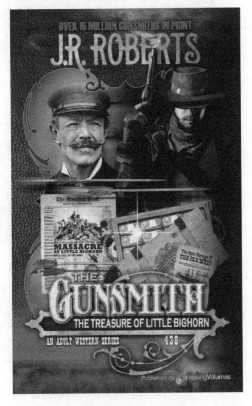

For more information
visit: www.speakingvolumes.us

On Sale Now!

THE GUNSMITH
436

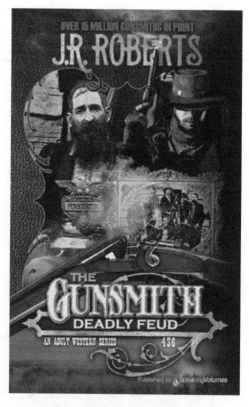

**For more information
visit:** www.speakingvolumes.us

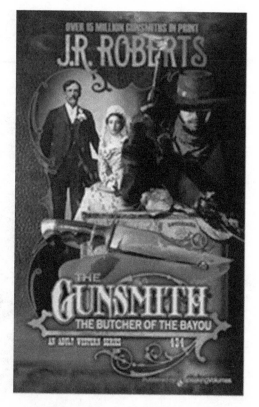

On Sale Now!

THE GUNSMITH
433

For more information
visit: www.speakingvolumes.us

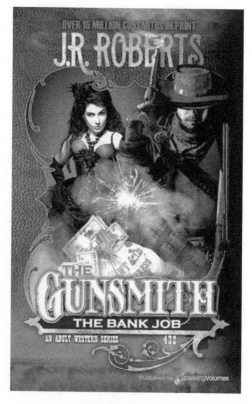

On Sale Now!

THE GUNSMITH
431

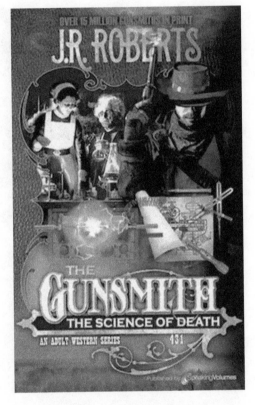

For more information
visit: www.speakingvolumes.us

On Sale Now!

THE GUNSMITH
430

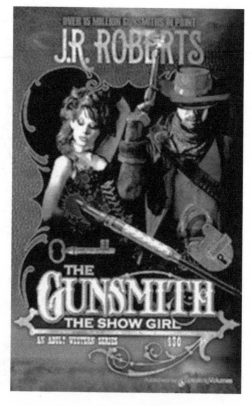

For more information
visit: www.speakingvolumes.us

On Sale Now!

**Lady Gunsmith 5
The Portrait of Gavin Doyle**

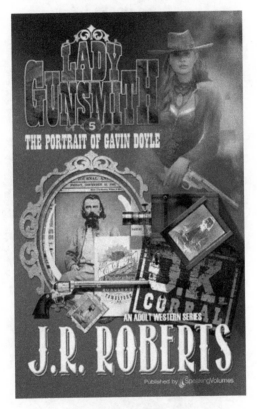

**For more information
visit:** www.speakingvolumes.us

On Sale Now!

Lady Gunsmith
A New Adult Western Series
Books 1-4

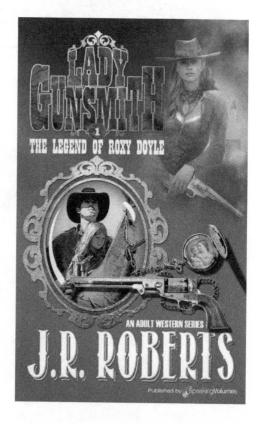

Roxanne Louise Doyle is Lady Gunsmith,
a hot, sexy woman who is unmatched with a gun...

For more information
visit: www.speakingvolumes.us

On Sale Now!

ANGEL EYES *series*
by
Award-Winning Author
Robert J. Randisi (J.R. Roberts)

For more information
visit:

On Sale Now!

TRACKER *series*
by
Award-Winning Author
Robert J. Randisi (J.R. Roberts)

On Sale Now!

MOUNTAIN JACK PIKE *series*
by
Award-Winning Author
Robert J. Randisi (J.R. Roberts)

For more information
visit: www.speakingvolumes.us